THE MINISTERS FAMILY GROWS

BY

RITA MUFF

To Kath with love from Rita Muff

Also by Rita Muff:

'The Minister's Family' 2012

'The Cotton King' 2013

All are available from Amazon

COPYRIGHT © 2013 Rita Muff

ISBN: 978-1-291-49493-8

All rights reserved.

No part of this book may be used or reproduced in any form whatsoever, or any electronic or mechanical means, including photocopying, recording or by any information storage or retrieval system, except in the case of brief quotations embodied in critical articles and reviews - without written permission of the author

This book is a work of fiction. The characters, places and incidents portrayed are fictitious or are used fictitiously. Any similarity to actual events or locales or persons, living or dead, is entirely coincidental and not intended by the author.

ACKNOWLEDGEMENTS

This book is dedicated to my husband Peter, our lovely family, and our many friends.

I would like to thank Jill Tucker and John Bell for proof reading, and our son-in-law Ian Carroll for arranging to publish this book, also to Peter for his help with computing skills. Any errors however are my responsibility.

All the characters in this book exist only in my imagination, and bear no likeness to any known person any similarity to anyone living or dead is entirely coincidental and not intended.

Though fictional, the story is typical of life in a Methodist Manse in the 1980's

Any profits from the sale of this book will be donated to the UK Charity 'Breast Cancer Care.'

PREFACE

This book follows on from, 'The Minister's Family' which told the story of The Rev. John Williams and his first Superintendency post in the early eighties.

John lives in a village called Cotteswold on the outskirts of Gloucester with his wife Anne. Their three grown-up children are Peter John, a bank manager who lives with his wife Vanessa and little daughter Emma in Weston-Super-Mare, Nicholas David, affectionately known as Nick, a music teacher, keen Arsenal supporter and ornithologist who lives in London, and Charlotte Anne who works as a House Mother for the National Children's Home caring for handicapped children in Birmingham. Charlotte Anne's husband is Richard a surgeon, and her twin girls Elizabeth and Rebecca are the proud owners of Sheltie dogs, Toffee and Fudge.

John's manse is an old Victorian town house next door to the church. In the first book falling numbers initially threatened the church with closure, but to the horror of many villagers a new housing estate was built on the outskirts of the village. Many new families attended the church, and instead of facing closure it expanded.

You can find out more about John's first year in Cotteswold in the first book 'The Minister's Family.'

CHAPTER ONE

It is hard to believe that we have only been in Cotteswold for a year. So much has happened, and we know a lot more people; some who will become life-long friends.

On 12th September Elizabeth and Rebecca became pupils at The Cathedral School and they were very excited about it. They had arranged to meet their friends, Katy and Sammy, in the car park, and indeed they were both standing waiting for us as we drew up at 8.45 am. New girls were shepherded into the hall by a member of staff, and they waved good-bye with happy faces.

John had a staff meeting in his study at 9.30 am, so we drove straight back home where I set about organising coffee and biscuits, whilst John prepared for his meeting. Later, when I was doing the housework, I could hear lots of happy laughter coming from the study, and I wondered if I would find out what it was all about. Sometimes I do, but very often I don't.

People often wonder what the Circuit Ministers talk about. Often it is about the maintenance of buildings, either churches or manses. Most of the churches are somewhere around a century old and need a lot of maintenance. This is, of course, very costly, and funds have to be raised to pay for them. These things have to be discussed with the Circuit Stewards. We are very lucky in this Circuit to have such excellent men; and they are all men. Norman Branston is a retired Solicitor and he and his wife Margery, who is also a local preacher and an organist, do an awful lot for us, and the circuit. Bob Diamond is the County Surveyor and a very busy man, yet he and his wife Valerie, also give their time to the Circuit. The other Steward is also Circuit Treasurer. Richard James is a Bank Manager and a very useful man. His wife Jane, is a great help in the Circuit, and is District Women's Meeting Secretary. They are a very able set of stewards, as well as being lovely helpful people. We are indeed very fortunate, and I know John is very grateful for their expertise as well as their support.

Another reason for staff meetings is for ministers to discuss pastoral problems, although all are very conscious of the need for confidentiality. It is often the problem, not the people, which is discussed. Ministers also need pastoral care, just like everyone else, and this is an opportunity to share their own concerns with their colleagues.

I know that many are intrigued with John's 'Talent Scheme.' This was begun last year when John preached about talents and then offered a 'bag of gold,' actually a five pound note in an envelope. People who accepted the challenge were asked to use their talents to make the five pounds into as much as they could, and bring it to Harvest Festival in October. All this money would be put into 'The Building Fund.'

We knew people were working very hard and there had been a lot of ingenuity and fun, as well as hard work. Just how much had been made we would only know at Harvest, when there would be a special collection for 'Talent Money.'

The telephone interrupted the meeting, which was nothing unusual. What was unusual was that John came to find me looking very upset.

"Anne, where are you?" he called. I came downstairs and knew by John's face this was something serious. "It's Irene," he said.

Irene had been busy about the house and Alf had fallen asleep in his chair. All perfectly normal. Since his heart attack last year Alf was, much to his disgust, a semi-invalid. This morning Irene had taken him his morning coffee and failed to wake him. She had rung John, because she was in absolute shock and didn't know what to do.

"I'll have to go straight away," John said. "Are you coming?"

"Yes, of course" I said, "but what about your meeting?"

"Alan will take over, and lock up when they are finished. He said he would put the key back through the letter box."

"All right," I said, "just give me a minute to turn the oven off." Then we were on our way.

We were soon with Irene, and when she opened the door we could see she was in shock. She simply said,

"He's lying back in the chair as if he's asleep, but I think he's gone." We all went into the lounge and saw Alf in his chair, looking very peaceful, but obviously dead. We sat down on the settee with Irene between us. She was trembling. John looked at me and I knew he was saying, "get a hot drink." When I took three mugs of tea in on a tray, John got up and went to telephone Alf's doctor, who was also our doctor. When John came back in he said, "He will be here as soon as he can." Whilst we drank our tea Irene said, "he was perfectly normal this morning. I helped him shower as usual, and he told me which clothes he wanted. He had his normal breakfast, just cereals and toast and marmalade. He dried up for me, and then sat down with his paper. The only unusual thing, when I think about it, was that he looked up at me and smiled and said, "I love you darling." He didn't often do that. Do you think he knew? The next thing I heard was his paper slip to the floor. But that wasn't unusual either, in fact it often happened, so why did I go in this time? All I could think of was, I must tell John. I'm so sorry, you must have been busy."

"I'm glad you rang me" John assured her. "You did exactly the right thing. What do you think I am here for?"

The doorbell rang and I got up to answer it. It was Dr. Bennett. He came into the lounge and went straight to Alf. He was only a few minutes before he said.

"I'm sorry Mrs. Davies, but I'm sure you know he has gone." Irene just nodded and wiped her eyes. Dr. Bennett wrote out a death certificate and said

"I'm sure you know we have to have another doctor to confirm the death, but the undertaker will see to all that." Then he kindly asked if she knew whom she wanted and whether she would like him to inform someone. Irene looked pleadingly at John and he said.

"It's very kind of you, but I'll see to everything for her and let Evan know about his Dad."

"You know it makes such a difference when patients belong to a church. They have the support that other people don't," he said. Then he left.

John asked Irene to give him Evan's telephone number and then asked her if she knew which Funeral Director she would want.

"I'll show you where Evan's number is" she said, "and I would like Bill to look after Alf. We had discussed it you know. After Alf's scare last year we decided to talk about both our deaths, and what we wanted to happen." Bill was a member of one of our churches, and he was Manager of the largest firm of Funeral Directors in Gloucester.

John was able to contact Evan quite quickly for he had rung his school. Evan was Deputy Head at a Grammar School in Reading. He was shocked, but not altogether surprised.

"I've been expecting something like this to happen since Dad had his heart attack. Trust him to pick the first day back after the long holidays. I'll be with Mum as soon as I can. Is she up to talking to me?"

John came back to Irene and asked her if she felt she could talk to her son.

"Oh yes, I've got to be brave, and if I break down it doesn't matter does it?"

"Of course not" John assured her "Evan will understand." Evan told his Mother he would be with her as soon as possible. "Pack a case," he said "and I'll bring you back with me."

"Oh not yet," Irene said, "I must be here to arrange things. After the funeral I'll be glad to come back with you for a few days break."

Evan told his Mother that she would be very welcome to make her home with them if she would like that.

"Oh no" Irene told him. "After a few days I will come back here and settle down to a different life, like lots of others have to, you know." Then she came back into the lounge and told us what Evan had offered.

"I love them all very much, but they have their lives to live and I have mine. All my friends and interests are here, and Alf and I both decided that that was what we wanted to do; although Alf knew if he were left he wouldn't be able to manage. He told me he would go into 'The Elms.' a Methodist Home for the Aged.

"If they'll have you?" I told him. Then she broke down and sobbed in my arms. I tried to get her to lie down on her bed, but she couldn't face that.

"We were there together a few hours ago," she sobbed.

The next ring at the bell proved to be Bill and his helpers. They were very kind and gentle with Alf's body.

"Take her away for a few minutes" Bill said. We gently led Irene into the kitchen whilst they saw to Alf's body. When they took him away Irene asked to go with him.

"You just give us an hour or two, then you can come and see him and stay as long as you like, until his funeral," Bill assured her.

Bill asked John when that would be likely to be, but John said they couldn't make any plans until Evan was here.

"Then," he said, "we will arrange things to suit everyone."

Evan arrived quicker than any of us thought possible and we were very glad to see his wife was with him. Megan was from 'The Valleys' and a very sweet and gentle person. Evan explained that when he had told his Headmaster, instead of having to arrange cover for his lessons, the Head said.

"Leave all that to me, off you go. Just let me know what's happening." Evan had taken him at his word and left the school. He called to pick up Megan, who made arrangements for the children with her sister, and they were on their way. They came by motorway and in less than two hours were with Irene.

We stayed just long enough to explain what had happened and John said he would ring later in the day. Then we left. Of course it was lunchtime, and no lunch was ready.

John said, "Well, I feel a bit empty, and I'm sure you do. Let's go to 'The Basket Maker' and have a quick lunch." I thought it was a good idea and it would save scratching around for something and then having to wash up. I had to collect the girls, and John had a Women's Meeting at 3 o'clock.

We both ordered soup and a ploughman's, and had just sat down when one of our church members came over to our table.

"Well," she said, "fancy seeing you in here. I didn't think you would have time to gad about." I was quite cross, but John pressed my knee gently under the table.

"The truth is Doreen, it's the only way either of us could have lunch today. We are just too busy."

She said "Oh I'm so sorry," and left in quite a hurry.

We went home to find the key behind the door and in his study John found a note from Alan giving him details of the rest of the meeting. I had a lovely surprise when I went into the kitchen to clear up. Everything was washed up and they had left the kitchen tidy. How kind of them.

John went to his meeting and I went to collect the girls. They came out beaming and pushed their school bags into the boot. Then Elizabeth stared at me

"What's happened?" she said looking very worried.

"It's Nana, isn't it?" cried Rebecca.

"No it isn't, it's Alf," I told them. "How did you know?"

"Just your face" they said together.

"Well, please get in the car and when we get home I'll tell you all about it." I promised. They jumped in and never said a word until we were home and in the kitchen.

"Now" they said together.

"Alf died very suddenly this morning." I explained, and they both burst into tears. I took them into the lounge and sat them down with a drink and a biscuit. Then I explained what had happened and that Evan and Megan were with Irene.

Both girls were very upset. They were very fond of Alf.

Then Rebecca said, "I don't know how you would know someone is dead. They might just be asleep."

I explained that there was a big difference.

"Somehow their personality has gone. All that is left is a shell."

"I know," said Elizabeth "like that chrysalis we found in the garage when the butterfly had flown."

"Exactly like that" I assured them.

"In my father's house are many mansions," quoted Rebecca. "Is that where Alf has gone?"

"Yes Rebecca, it is," I said, "and that is why that portion of scripture is usually read at funerals."

"So where exactly is Alf now?" asked Elizabeth.

"Well," I answered, "his body is at the Funeral Parlour, but his soul is in heaven."

"How on earth is anyone supposed to know the way to Heaven?" asked Rebecca.

"I can only tell you what I believe happens" I said. "I have been with several people when they have died, and all of them have seen a loved one who has died previously. Some just smile, some say a name. I was with my Auntie Fie when she died and she definitely saw her Mother who had died twenty years before. She called her Mum, and held her hand out to her and smiled. Yes I am quite convinced that our nearest and dearest come to collect us."

"If you say someone we love comes to collect us, then we are still alive, but in a different way. Is that what you mean?"

"Yes it is Elizabeth."

"But I don't see that." Elizabeth shook her head.

"Neither can I" agreed her twin. "How can you be alive in a different way?"

"But my loves, you have already experienced that" I smiled. "We all have, although we don't of course remember."

"What on earth do you mean?" they answered together. I put my arms around both of them, and tried to explain.

"The day before you two were born," I smiled, "you were definitely alive, I could feel you moving about inside me and the nurse could hear your hearts beating. There is no doubt you were alive, but in a totally different way. You were not able to breathe for instance; you didn't need food and drink, yet you were alive, only in a different dimension. Then you were born and took your first breath. You were now in the world, in a totally different way, do you understand?"

"Golly I never thought of that," said Elizabeth, and Rebecca said,

"I'm going to my room to have a good think."

"Now," I said, "Alf wouldn't want you to be unhappy about him. Dry your eyes and remember him as he was. All we can do for him now, is to look after Irene when she comes back from Reading."

"Do we have to go to the funeral?" asked Elizabeth.

"Definitely not." I said. "You will be at school, and talking of school, how did it go?"

They both cheered up and told me all about it. They were in Plantagenet House. "We call it Plan, and we have a yellow badge." They showed me, it was pinned onto their grey jumpers.

"We are in form 1A and our teacher is called Mrs.Day. She is lovely, but we only saw her for registration and she took us to assembly. Then the English teacher took us back to our form room and our first lesson was writing out our timetable. Then we were taken to the mathematics room and told we were never to call it maths. Then it was break and we went out into the grounds for twenty minutes. After that we had history. Our history teacher came to collect us from the garden and took us into a room in the old building. She told us about the history of the Manor House. Then it was lunchtime, and we all went into first lunch. The older girls, form four and above have second lunch. During lunch break we could choose: we could just play or we could go to one of the lunchtime activities. Rebecca chose the Gym Club and I chose music. In the afternoon we had music and art. Then it was home time."

"But we have home-work to do," said Rebecca. They were in the same form as their friends and were therefore perfectly happy. I suggested they get out of their uniforms and hang them up tidily.

"Then you can put your jeans and tee shirts on and play until teatime." They scurried off and were their cheerful selves again.

John came in from his meeting and heard all about school; with a few extras such as what societies they could join. They both wanted 'Drama' and that was included in their Scholarship. Both would like to join the School Choir and Orchestra, and Rebecca said she would like Gym Club. She fancied the trampoline. We said we would talk about it and see what could be managed. With this they were quite content.

CHAPTER TWO

Alf's funeral took place during the next week. The church was full to overflowing and there were many tributes paid to him. It helped his family to know what a very good friend he had been to so many people. He had requested that there should be family flowers only, but any donations should be for his beloved church. Irene said it must go to the Building Fund.

"He was very keen on this project," she said.

A short service at the crematorium followed, but only family and close friends were asked to attend.

Everyone else was invited to 'Alf's party' in the schoolroom. Irene's friends had arranged it all, and what a spread there was. It was in full swing when the family returned. Irene told us that it all helped her to get through the day. She was going back with Evan and Megan. The children had not come to the funeral and were being looked after by their auntie in Reading.

"They are too young to understand" Irene said, "and their Grandpa would not want them to be upset." Rhiannon is only six and her little brother Alwyn, is not quite four. They have been told that their Grandpa has gone to live with Jesus, and they have accepted that."

Irene was away for about ten days and she rang us when she returned.

"Can I come and see you both?" she asked.

"No," said John, "we will come and see you." We went to her house the next afternoon, and she told us that whilst she was away she thought about her future.

"Do you think Granny Donkersley would like to come and live with me?" she asked. "She really shouldn't be living alone, and I would love to have her. We have always been good friends, and I would be lonely here on my own. What do you think?"

John and I looked at each other and smiled. It would certainly solve a problem. We were worried, like many people, that Granny Donkersley would not be able to cope alone much longer. But she is far too independent to go into a home.

"Invite her for a cup of tea and tell her you are lonely" suggested John, "but have you thought about the arrangements you would have to make?"

"Oh yes, I have" she smiled. "You see we have the dining room behind the kitchen, come and see."

We went with her and found a beautiful sunny room overlooking the garden. Outside was a patio with garden furniture and a bird table.

"What a lovely room," I said "It's just right for Granny D." Then she opened a door and showed us the toilet, washbasin, and a shower.

"We had this put in for Alf" Irene said. John and I nodded.

"Perfect for Granny D."

"By the way," I said, "Granny D must have a name, but we all call her Granny D."

"Oh yes, she is Hannah Grace Donkersley."

"What a beautiful name," I said, "and it just suits her."

"Do as I suggest," smiled John, "but don't be upset if she refuses. She may well."

Then it was time to collect the girls and John had another appointment with Bill to arrange yet another funeral. This was for someone we didn't know and therefore much easier. John had found Alf's service very difficult to get through. People don't realise how emotional it is for a minister when the person being committed is also a friend. Everyone else can wipe their eyes, but not the minister, he, or she, just has to keep going. Perhaps only I know how difficult it is, and that is how it should be.

When the girls came out of school they were very excited. In their drama lesson Mrs. Hazelbury had read them the play they were to present at the beginning of December. It was 'Alice in Wonderland' and next week they were going to read the parts through. Then would come the excitement of learning lines and practising the play.

This was to be a Junior School production, so only first, second, and third forms would perform it. Of course everyone would want to be Alice. She must not only look the part, but also have a good speaking voice and be able to sing. There was much chatter on the way home. Then Elizabeth remembered to tell me that Sammy's Mum wanted me to ring her when we got home. I rang whilst it was fresh in my mind and she came up with the idea that we should share the driving. Katy's Mum was also keen. We met to discuss a plan that would save us all a lot of time. In the end we agreed that we would do the school run for a week, and then have two weeks off.

We decided to begin right away. I would do the first week, then Katy's Mum followed by Sammy's Mum. This was a wonderful help and we all agreed that if there was a problem so one of us couldn't do our run, we would just ring one of the others and swop a turn.

Guides were doing very well under their new Captain, and Jane was thoroughly enjoying it. She was also enjoying her baby, Beth, who was a very contented baby. The formal adoption was booked and was only three weeks away. As soon as they knew the date Jane had rung to book her baptism.

"She is to be Bethany Anne, and John has agreed that as well as baptising her, he will also be her only godfather. You and Elizabeth and Rebecca have already agreed to be her godmothers, so she should be well cared for."

This was a great joy to all of us. Baby Beth was doing well for a little girl with Downs Syndrome. She was certainly getting lots of attention and stimulation. Our girls were very proud to be her godmothers and had bought her a Mrs. Tiggywinkle mobile to hang over her cot. John and I bought her a Beatrix Potter feeding dish and mug. We were all looking forward to her baptism.

Granny Donkersley asked John and me to go and have a cup of tea with her as soon as we had time.

"Something rather wonderful has happened," she smiled, and we didn't spoil it all for her by saying we could guess.

We sat around her table enjoying her wonderful shortbread and a huge coffee and walnut cake.

"I have been getting quite worried," she said. "I would hate having to go into a home. How would I be able to make things like this?" she said, spreading her arms around the table, "and yet I know I can't go on too much longer by myself. My children have both offered to have me. They said I would live a few months with each. I know I would be loved and cared for, but they have busy lives and I couldn't be part of that. I wouldn't know anyone who would come and chat to me. I love my grandchildren dearly, but they are always rushing about doing all sorts of things. It would never do, and I would soon be worn out. I have prayed about it and asked for help. Then Irene came to see me and offered me a home with her. Talk about an answer to prayer," she smiled. "She even said it would help her because she was feeling lonely without Alf."

"This is wonderful news" John smiled, and we both gave her a hug.

"I have been to see the room I would have. It overlooks the garden and is very bright and sunny. Irene has kindly said I can take my own bed and my chair. She even said that I must treat the whole house as my home and only go to my room when I want to. She is so understanding."

"Well," John said, "you are both very excited about all this. When exactly is it going to happen?"

"Definitely before Christmas," Granny smiled, "but I have to dispose of this house somehow. Irene suggests I put it up for sale and move in with her in the meantime. I have been thinking about it. Then my son came up with a suggestion. They love this area and so does my daughter, so why don't I just move in with Irene and they will use it as a holiday cottage. I think I might accept that. All the furniture would be here; except my bed and chair. My family will see to what they need. All I would need to do is pack my clothes and Ted has offered to help with getting me moved in. What do you think?"

We both thought it was a marvellous idea.

"Ted also said he would keep the grass cut and the garden tidy. Isn't that kind of him?"

"Well what are you waiting for?" asked John.

"Just your approval" she smiled.

Irene was very thrilled about the arrangements.

"Everything will be there, so if Granny D has forgotten something she can simply go and get it," she said.

So everything was organised and Granny D and Irene would settle down together quite happily for the winter.

Our friend, Pam, was waiting to go into hospital. She was hoping that the surgeon would only need to remove the lump. That, however, depended on how far the cancer had spread. She had talked to a lady at 'Breast Cancer Care' and couldn't praise them enough.

"They have promised to be there for me whatever happens," she said.

I had promised to go with her to the hospital. "Derek is no use where anything medical is needed. He just feels sick and can't face it."

"Let's hope he never needs treatment himself" I smiled.

"I would never get him to admit he needed help that way," Pam said. Then she confided something to me.

"I'm sure he should see the doctor about a man's problem," she said. "Do you know he can't go much longer than an hour without going to the loo. He says he has a small bladder, but I wish he would go and see someone about it."

"Do you want me to tell John?" I asked.

"Yes, I think I do" she answered. "But I don't know what he can do about it."

"Oh John has ways and means" I said. "This won't be the first time he has dealt with this problem you know. Many men have the same reluctance to seek help. Derek is by no means the only one."

"All right" she said. "You have a word with John and see if he can be any help. He probably will listen to John. He thinks the world of him."

Pam had just left when the girls came bursting in from school.

"Mum, Mum, where are you?" I opened the kitchen door and came into the hall.

"What on earth?" I didn't get any further.

"We are Alice," they shouted.

"Come into the lounge and tell me, how can you both be Alice?"

"Well we are," they shouted. "We are taking two days each. Elizabeth is taking the part on Tuesday and Thursday and I am doing Wednesday and Friday," said Rebecca. What an excitement!

"Mrs. Hazelbury says we are a gift to her. It is such a big part, and she knew she would have to have two girls for four nights. So as we look exactly alike it's perfect. We had to audition at lunch time and Mrs. Hazelbury said we both read and sang beautifully and as long as we thought we could learn our lines we were the solution to her problem."

"Well this is all very exciting," I said. "Are you sure you can both learn the parts?"

"Of course" they both shouted. "We've already started learning and we know the first scene already."

"Goodness" I said. "Wait till Daddy comes in."

John of course was very pleased with them and said, "This deserves a treat. What's for dinner?"

"Cold meat and chips," I told him, "and I'd better get the oven on or there won't be that."

"Don't put the oven on at all. Get your coats and we'll go and have medieval fish and chips."

"Great" was the only response.

CHAPTER THREE

The first Sunday in October was the date set for our very special Harvest Festival. It was a beautiful autumn day and everyone was looking forward to it. There had been much speculation about how much 'Talent Money' had been made and we would soon find out. John had asked each talent holder to let our treasurer, Derek, know the amount they would be handing in, so this could be announced during the service.

Some time ago John had been looking for a suitable hymn that could be sung whilst the congregation processed up with their offerings. As so often happens, he just couldn't find anything appropriate. I was thinking about it, and trying to write one for him, when Babs, one of our members gave me the idea. Our organist had been very ill with kidney trouble and she was asking me how he was.

"He is often in pain" she said, "yet how he makes the organ sing."

Into my mind came the tune from 'Ode to Joy' "And some can make the organ sing." I thought of all the different talents that people in the church had used, and began.

"Lord the source of all our talents
Take our gratitude we pray
For the varied gifts and graces
Found within our church today
Some are artists, some musicians,
Others work with wood or clay.
May our gifts and all our talents
Glorify your name today.

Some bring talents to our worship
Worship fit for Christ our King
Some can preach, or teach, or write
And some can make the organ sing.
Some can read the scriptures clearly,

Serve communion, intercede
All sing hymns and share responses
Contribute to worshipping.

Lord we thank you for the talents
Used by some from week to week:
Those who please us all with flowers,
Those who take them to the sick;
Those who work to help the children,
Those who care for elderly,
Those who see the church is ready
For our worship, week by week.

None should feel they have no talent:
All can smile and be a friend;
Listen to another's problems;
Just be there in time of need.
Everybody's gifts are needed
So the church can do its work:
Help us all fulfil our mission
In the church and in the world."

John gave me a hug and said "Thanks love. It's exactly what I was looking for. We will sing it. I think it should go very well."

The only two people who knew what the final 'Talent Money' amounted to were John and Derek, and they were not breathing a word to anybody. The service began with the great Harvest hymn 'Come ye thankful people come.' They certainly had come. There were no spare seats and spare chairs were placed anywhere a chair would fit. Several people became agitated about safety, but John calmed them.

"I hardly think we need worry about fire since no-one will be smoking."

The church looked beautiful as it always did. Mum and Dad had come to stay to enjoy the service with us. Mum nudged me and grinned.

"No holy roses this year?"

John nodded to Derek and he came forward holding a large basket in his hand. John explained that we had had a hymn especially written for the occasion, and it was on the sheet provided. During the hymn we were asked to go forward a row at a time and take our envelopes containing our five-pound note and the extra we had made.

The hymn went very well and it had to be sung through again as there was still a queue when it ended. John then said a prayer of thanksgiving and gave out the amount raised. A stunned silence followed the announcement, followed by a great burst of applause.

Three thousand five hundred pounds had been raised. Fifty-two families had taken five pounds. So two hundred and sixty pounds had been given out. This meant that three thousand two hundred and forty pounds had been made for the 'Building Fund,' John then told them that just over one thousand pounds had also been given in memory of Alf. There was great cause for thanksgiving.

The next day was the 'Harvest Supper,' much the same as it had been a year ago. The only difference for us was that we knew nearly everyone there.

Granny D had already moved in with Irene and they both looked very happy about the arrangements. Ted had been a great help with getting Granny settled and attending to her garden. She insisted on paying him as her gardener, so Ted took it willingly and promptly handed it to Derek towards church funds. Everyone felt very satisfied.

Mum and Dad were very happy in 'Westerley,' and Chris, my brother, was taking them back at the end of the week. He also visited Jane and Bob and their family. He was delighted to see how happy they were with little Beth and amazed to see how responsive she was to them.

The whole family were very pleased that the twins were going to be 'Alice' and one and all demanded tickets. The girls assured them they would get them, but for which night? We decided that we would split the days so some would see Elizabeth and others Rebecca. On the night they were not taking the main part they had a small part, so were on the stage anyway.

We had a phone call from Charlotte Anne asking us to get tickets. They could only come on the Friday, as they had to work on the other days. We also had a letter from Carey Jane telling us how much she was enjoying her nursing training. She said she was thrilled that her little cousins had the leading part, and she would love to see them on stage. Carey is a leading member in a big drama group in Birmingham and we have often seen her in productions.

"I'm so glad my cousins are taking an interest in drama," she said.

"It's not the only thing either," said Elizabeth. "I hope to follow her into nursing."

"I don't," said Rebecca, "I would like to be a teacher."

"Well," I said, "there is no reason why you should not achieve your ambitions. It just means hard work for both of you."

"Do you know something?" said Elizabeth. "I'm finding it easier to work at The Cathedral School."

"That's funny," said Rebecca "So do I."

"Just keep it up" I smiled. "You both seem to have lots of 'house marks.'"

"Well we want Plan to get the cup," they said together. Then Elizabeth explained. At the end of the week the House Captain comes round the forms and asks our Form Captain how many house marks we have been awarded for our house. They are all counted up and at the end of term the cup is awarded to the house with most points.

"Points are awarded for lots of things besides work," Rebecca reminded her. "I got one for my swimming."

"And I got one because I helped one of the juniors. She is only four years old and she fell and hurt her knee in the playground. I took her into her teacher and she gave me a house point."

"Well done both of you." I smiled. "Just carry on the good work."

The next excitement was baby Beth's baptism. She had been legally adopted and could now be baptised. When John made the sign of the cross on her head she smiled at him as if she understood. Jane had asked if they could use the baptismal hymn, which I had written for Emma and of course, I agreed.

Jane had invited several of us to a buffet lunch afterwards, and it was lovely to see so many people admiring little Beth. She lapped it up and loved being passed around like a little parcel.

In November I had a surprise telephone call from the Headmistress at The Cathedral School.

"Which one?" I asked feeling very worried.

"Neither of them," she assured me. "In fact they have both been most helpful and I'm the one who is in trouble. You see, Mrs. Williams, four of my staff have this wretched flu virus. I explained to the girls in assembly what would have to happen. Immediately after assembly there was a knock on my door and your two girls stood there."

"Our Mummy is a teacher and we are sure she would come in and help," they said.

"So I am taking them at their word and pleading for help."

"Of course I will help" I said. "But I was in the middle of changing beds and I hardly look fit to stand in front of a class. If you give me half-an-hour I'll try and find out where my husband is, and get him to bring me in."

"I'm truly grateful," Mrs. Jenner answered. "Don't get into a hectic rush. If you could come in this afternoon it would be wonderful."

That I could promise, as John would be in about 12.30pm and I knew he would run me in to the school. That gave me time to collect my thoughts and change. I wondered what subjects I would be teaching and to what age group?

John was surprised, but he is used to sudden decisions and gladly agreed to take me in after lunch.

"I don't know about picking you up though?"

"That's all right," I said. "It's Katy's Mum's turn to pick the girls up and she will bring me back I'm sure."

John dropped me off at the school car park and went off to his meeting. I made my way to the office. The Secretary was expecting me and took me up to Mrs. Jenner's room. She greeted me warmly and thanked me for coming so quickly. Then she took out a huge timetable and scanned it.

"I can take sixth form Latin myself," she said. "What I wonder would you prefer? I can offer J2, who are all four or five years old. Fourth Form history, or Transition Form. They are all ten years old and this afternoon is mathematics, English literature, followed by R.E."

"Just what I would love," I smiled.

Mrs. Jenner took me to Transition form room, in the new building. She told me their reader was 'The Woolpack." I knew the book, and had in fact read it to my two a few months before.

She told me that they were reading this as a background to their geography for this term, which was 'The Wool Trade' she said. As we had reached the form room the fifteen girls stood up and said. "Good-afternoon Mrs. Jenner." Then she introduced me and they very politely said "Good Afternoon" to me.

"Do your best for Mrs. Williams" she said. "Alice is form captain and will help I know." She thanked the prefect who had been sitting with the girls. Then she left me with Transition form. Adele returned to the sixth form and I faced fifteen ten-year olds.

I asked who Alice was and she came forward. I noticed she was wearing a Tudor badge. She brought out her textbook and showed me what the form were working on. It was the very beginning of square numbers and square root. I thanked her and sent her back to her place.

"Now," I said, "how many of you are happy to continue with exercise one?" Only two hands went up so I decided a class lesson would be best. Several girls knew what a square number was, but some looked completely blank.

"Do we have any squared paper?" I asked. Alice came to me and showed me their mathematics exercise books. At the back was a section with quite a lot of squared paper.

"Right" I said. "Let's play a game." I told them to choose a number of squares in a line. "Not too many, and colour them in. Use your favourite colour."

They all looked very happy and I could see lots of tongues hung out. Then they sat up.

"Now," I said. Colour in the same number of squares down the page and tell me what shape you have made?"

Hands waved in the air and all of them were longing to tell me that it was a square.

"How many squares have you filled in?" I asked a girl sitting in the front row.

"Nine" she answered.

"Then that means you started with just three squares."

"How did you know?" She sounded very surprised.

"Because the square root of nine is three" I smiled. Then I showed them on the blackboard the sign for square root.

Some understood straight away, others looked puzzled.

"Can you square any number?" one girl asked.

"Try it, and see what happens." I suggested. Then I wrote some numbers on the board and suggested they write them in their rough books. Now try to find the square for each number. They quickly understood. Then I tried writing some numbers and asked them to find the square root. Most of them understood and quickly found the answers. Then for homework, I told them to write down the numbers two to twelve and put the square of each number beside it. They enjoyed the lesson and as they had all learned their tables long ago no one had a problem.

The bell rang and we changed to English literature. The girls quickly put their books away and took out their reader. 'The Wool-Pack' by Cynthia Harnett. A story about the wool trade in 1493 set in the Cotswolds. Their copies were beautifully illustrated. Alice showed me where they had got to in the book, and we all enjoyed reading Chapter Eleven about 'Cloth.' As many of the girls were farmers' daughters and some lived in the Cotswolds, it was very interesting for them to read about their ancestors.

There was a short break after the lesson, and the teacher in the next room came to take me to the staff room for a welcome cup of tea, whilst the girls took out bottles of juice from their bags and went off into the grounds for fifteen minutes.

The staff room was in the old house and looked out onto the gardens. Everyone enjoyed a cup of tea and a biscuit and there was a lot of chatter. I was introduced to several of the teachers and surprised to notice several men amongst the staff, although why I should be surprised I couldn't say. Mrs. Day came to speak to me and told me how immediately after prayers, both girls had suggested that I might be able to help, and she had sent them straight up to Mrs. Jenner's room.

"So glad you could help out" she smiled.

I walked back to Transition room with J4's teacher and found the girls all in their places waiting quietly for me. The last lesson for the afternoon was R.E., which I had studied for my main course when I was at college. The girls were studying the parables of Jesus and were about to begin 'The Good Samaritan.' I asked if they had ever acted any of the parables. They hadn't, so I suggested they might like to try, and asked for volunteers. A sea of hands greeted me and I chose a few girls to take the parts and we acted it with Alice as narrator. Then I asked a few questions and they gave me quite thoughtful answers. I told them to think about 'being a good neighbour' and write a few notes on what Jesus meant by saying it was 'The Samaritan' who was the good neighbour.

Then the bell rang for the end of school and there was Mrs. Jenner at the door waiting for me.

She said. "Elizabeth and Rebecca have been told to go to my room to wait for you. Shall we go up?"

Katie had been told to tell her Mum that Mrs. Jenner would take us home, so that was all right.

We arrived at Mrs. Jenner's room and the girls were waiting for us. We all went in and she told the twins that I had been most helpful and how pleased she was that they had suggested me.

"Now I don't know how long it will be before Mrs. Warren is fit again,

or any of the others for that matter. If you can possibly help us for a few days I would be most grateful."

I quickly thought of what was on the calendar in the next few days. I told Mrs. Jenner that I would help where I could, but I had promised Pam I would take her for a hospital appointment and I wouldn't let her down. Mrs. Jenner understood and said she would appreciate any time I could give her. She kindly drove us home, and I said I would definitely be able to do full time the next day and I would let her know then about the rest of the week.

The twins were quite excited about me teaching in their school.

Elizabeth said, "I don't know about you teaching us though."

"Definitely not" announced Rebecca. "It would be awful to call you Mrs. Williams." Then we all laughed.

"Drink and something to eat" I said. "Then get changed and do your homework, whilst I look at this timetable for tomorrow. I'd better be prepared myself."

John came in later to find all his women folk busy with homework. I would have mathematics, English and geography in the morning and P.E, drama and music in the afternoon. All the afternoon, specialist teachers took the subjects, so I would not be needed. Maths and English were no problem, but geography was not a favourite with me. Then I remembered that Mrs. Jenner had explained that their reader 'The Woolpack' was to tie in with their geography. The 'Wool Trade' held no terrors for me so I would be all right with that.

Pam's hospital appointment was the next afternoon at 3 o'clock and I had already arranged with John to have the car so it would all work out all right. The only thing I had to worry about was the housework. That would just have to wait.

I rang Mrs. Jenner and told her I would be all right for the morning and the rest of the week. She was very relieved that the hospital appointment could be accommodated.

I enjoyed the rest of the week. Pam's hospital appointment was not at all traumatic, and she told me she had found 'Breast Cancer Care' a great help. "I have someone I can talk to about anything that is worrying me and they seem to understand. They are so helpful" she said.

I told Pam how much I was enjoying teaching again and she laughed when I said, "housework will just have to wait until the weekend."

"Oh no it won't," she smiled, "what I am I here for?"

"Do you really mean it? You would come and do the housework?"

"Of course," she said. "You wouldn't need me every day would you?"

"Gracious no," I answered. "We can all manage the day-to-day work between us. If you could come once a week and what my Mum calls 'bottom' everywhere that would be marvellous." We agreed on a 'rate of pay' although Pam refused at first. I told her I would be paid for the hours I taught and would not agree unless she accepted payment. We were both happy about it. Pam would come on Friday morning and stay as long as necessary.

"I'll leave John a light lunch if you leave something suitable in the fridge" she said.

So for the next two weeks I worked full time at The Cathedral School and Pam, bless her, made the house sparkle.

Mrs. Jenner spoke to me one day in the Staff Room.

"The children tell me you are brilliant at explaining difficult parts of mathematics," she said.

"I don't know about that," I answered, "but I enjoy unravelling them."

"Now that does need an explanation," she laughed.

"Well," I explained, "I love knitting, but if the pattern goes wrong there is nothing to do but unravel it and start again. That is what I explained to some of Transition. A few of them were in a complete mess with fractions and decimals, so I told them the best thing to do was to unravel them and start again. I'm afraid I use Smarties as a bit of bribery. It works wonders."

"Well I have one or two older girls who also need unravelling," she smiled. "How would you like a permanent job?"

I was astonished and told her I would have to think about it, and talk it over with John. Filling in for a week or two was wonderful, but full time? Would that be possible? I went back to Transition with my mind in a whirl. What would the family think?

John was surprised but said, "It's entirely up to you. Would you like it?"

"I would love it," I said, "but how about the church? What would they think?" John thought for a moment and then smiled at me.

"The church employ me, and I will still do my job. They do not employ you. You are just as entitled to work as any other church member. Lots of our Mums work and still do their bit in the church, why not you?"

We talked it over with the girls when we were having our evening meal. Elizabeth, ever practical, said

"What about the car?"

John agreed that he would not always be available to take us, nor to pick us up.

Then he said "If you are a full time teacher, and getting full pay, then we can easily afford a car for you."

"Brilliant," answered Rebecca. "Then you will be able to run us around."

I rang Mrs. Jenner, as she had asked me to, and she was delighted that I felt able to work full time on a permanent basis. She explained that she would have to consult the governors. She also asked me to let the Bursar have the details of my qualifications and previous experience. For the next week I was to spend my time with Transition form and give extra lessons to older girls when Transition were with other teachers. There were quite a few periods when this was possible. As well as music, drama and art they had specialist teachers for science and P.E.

I was introduced to Jane, who was in the sixth form and specialising in drama, two fifth form girls who just needed a little individual attention with mathematics, and a group of girls from the first year who had not reached the same standard as the rest.

John and I had sorted out problems like shopping, which I had always done, and a very big problem 'answering the telephone.' We agreed that we would do the shopping together on Saturday mornings. But the telephone? John liked to spend the morning in his study, if possible. Afternoons he was never at home for that was when he did some of his visiting, especially at the hospital, the schools or the residential homes. This was going to be a problem.

Then Elizabeth said, "Why not buy an answer phone?" Problem solved, or so we thought.

CHAPTER FOUR

I was thoroughly enjoying my teaching. Most problems seemed to be sorting themselves out. We were looking for a small car when Irene solved our problem in a wonderful way.

"John," she said. "You offered to help me in any way you possibly could.

"Yes" he assured her.

"Well Alf's car is my biggest problem. It's getting to a stage where I don't want to go into the garage. I'm avoiding it as much as possible. Would you please come and take it away? Would it be any use to you?" John was staggered.

"Irene," he said, "Alf's car, if I remember correctly is a fairly new Datsun Bluebird and worth quite a bit. Do you mean you would like me to sell it for you?"

"Oh no" she smiled. "Evan and I have been trying to think of something which belonged to Alf, which would be useful to you. We are just so grateful for all you have done. We both thought of the car. We know Alf would be thrilled to know you were driving it, and finding it useful. What do you think?"

"I am astonished," John answered. "Of course I would love to have Alf's car and it truly would be a Godsend. But I must give you something for it."

"Oh no" that wouldn't do at all. Alf would be most upset. It must be a gift."

"Well then, what can I say but a big Thank You and I will write to Evan and tell him so. There is just one thing I must know, and that is how you are going to feel when you see me driving it when I am out and about, and you are not expecting it."

Irene thought about it for a few minutes and then smiled,

"Comforted," she said.

I was as surprised as John and just as delighted. Alf was very proud of his car and kept it in excellent order.

I drove John to Irene's house and after a cup of tea with her and Granny D, she gave John the keys for his new car and told him the garage was open, and she would be glad to see the back of it. She also handed John a large envelope.

"Evan says you must have these documents. It's all to do with car insurance. And by-the-way Alf was insured for any other driver to drive his car, so that's all right. I believe you have to let some authority know that it is now your car. Evan has written a note to anyone concerned, letting them know the car now belongs to you."

It was a lovely car, far better than anything we could have afforded, and a delightful shade of blue, rather like a summer sky.

We soon got into a regular routine. The girls and I left the house at 8 15.am. and arrived home about 4 15.pm. Of course I had to spend part of the evening marking and preparing lessons, but this was not causing any problems. I prepared our evening meal before I left in the morning and set the washing machine going. Pam came in twice a week. Monday morning she did ironing and the bedrooms. Friday she spent on the rest of the house, and cleaned out the fridge or kitchen drawers and the pantries.

On Saturday mornings after shopping I baked cakes, biscuits and sometimes meals to go in the freezer. We were always busy, but what was different? The biggest problem was that I was not available during the day if anyone from church wanted me.

Someone had tackled John about this.

"Suppose someone wants to talk to a woman about a personal matter?" she asked. John explained that I was still available in the evenings.

"Oh yes," the lady said "but some of us like to see her in the afternoons."

"Well, if that is the case," John said, "perhaps the church will have to employ someone."

"Oh dear me no. We couldn't afford that," she said.

"So what you are saying," John smiled "is that you want two of us for the price of one?"

When John was telling me about this, he said

"Now don't go feeling guilty about it. They don't know what they are implying."

"Who was it?" I asked. When he told me I laughed, "but she was a Head Mistress."

"Exactly." John laughed.

My wages at the end of the month were a great help. We are not exactly poor, but we do have to be very careful. John, like all Methodist Ministers is paid quarterly. On the 1st September, December, March and June, and it has to last until the next payday. We do not have a mortgage or rent to pay, but we live in a larger house than people on his salary would normally have, and that means bigger bills, for lighting, heating, water and so on.

My wages would certainly mean life was a little easier. The other thing we thought we could do was to allow the girls to join more societies. Elizabeth would like a violin and Rebecca really longed for a flute. Neither is cheap. Rebecca also fancied the trampoline. We could certainly afford that now. Both girls joined the choir and junior orchestra and they both enjoyed swimming.

The school production was a great success. Both girls played their parts to perfection and we were all very proud of them. Elizabeth, remembering the dress rehearsal for 'The Most Beautiful Story of All' last year, suggested to Mrs. Hazlebury that the children from the 'Special School' should be invited. Mrs. Hazlebury was delighted and asked permission to invite them to come to an afternoon performance, especially put on for them. They came and thoroughly enjoyed themselves.

John could only manage one evening but I went to all of the performances and took Pam and Derek along with me to the first night. Granny D and Irene came one evening and thoroughly enjoyed it. Charlotte Anne and Richard came on the last night. Both Alice's were brought to the front and applauded. The hall was full and everyone enjoyed it. Charlotte Anne was very proud of her sisters and so was Carey Jane who had also managed to come for the last performance. She is thoroughly enjoying her nursing training and I'm sure she will make a wonderful nurse.

Christmas was not far away and this year we were having a complete change. One of the Circuit Ministers had suggested at a staff meeting that it would be a good idea to have a Circuit service on Christmas morning. They had talked it over and decided to put it to the Circuit Meeting that there should be one Christmas Eve midnight communion in one church, and a morning service in another church on Christmas Day. The idea was accepted, with some reluctance, and two churches were suggested. This meant John was free this year and we could accept an invitation from our Yorkshire family to spend Christmas with them.

We would have our family get together in the New Year. We arranged to travel up to Yorkshire on Christmas Eve and come back the day after Boxing Day. Nick would come with us. Peter John and his family were spending Christmas with Vanessa's parents and Charlotte Anne and Richard were going to his Mum and Dad. My parents were very happy to spend Christmas at 'Westerley.' All fitted in quite nicely and everyone looked forward to it.

I still had lots of shopping to do of course, and I wondered whether we had better book Toffee and Fudge into kennels. However, Pam asked if she and Derek could have them to stay with them. "We would love to have them and they do know us. It wouldn't be such a stress for them or for you." The girls especially were delighted. They did not want them to go into kennels. So all seemed to be sorting out very well.

One or two people in the church grumbled about not having us around at Christmas, but we needed the break.

Term ended on 18th December and the new term began on January 12th. This meant there was time to plan and organise a family day as well as our church 'Thank You' buffet.'

Another piece of good news was that the Shepherdesses were having Dulcie's son and his family for a visit over the New Year. They were to have bed and breakfast at the village inn, and spend the rest of the time with the three sisters. Now Dulcie could proudly take them to morning service and let everyone meet them. It was quite an experience for her and she thoroughly enjoyed it. They were a family anyone could be proud of and they enjoyed their time with us. The children called Dulcie Granny Shepherd and she delighted in her new family.

We were all packed up ready to go off to Yorkshire when Nick arrived. He just had time to admire the new car, have a drink and then we were off. We would stop on the motorway for lunch and hope to arrive in Illingworth about 3 o'clock, just before it got dark.

On the way Nick turned round. He had been sitting beside John, and I was in the middle of the girls in the back seat. He beamed at us and said.

"I've got some news for you. I've met a lovely girl called Caroline."

"This is good news," John smiled whilst the twins called out

"Whoopee, and is this another wedding coming?" I just smiled and patted his back.

"Tell us more, where did you meet?"

"On the football terrace," he grinned. "She is a great Arsenal supporter. She has a season ticket and follows them to all their matches, even abroad."

"Goodness," I smiled at him, "I would have said you were an all-out supporter. She sounds just right for you. What does she look like, what is her name, and how old is she?"

"Well here is a picture of us taken last week on the terraces by a mutual friend." He showed us a picture of them both in Arsenal kit and looking very happy. She was as tall as Nick and looked a very nice girl.

"Tell us more," I said. "Firstly what is her name?"

"Caroline Davidson, and by the way, it's Caroline to rhyme with time, never call her Caroline to rhyme with tin."

"Where does she work?" Elizabeth asked.

"She is secretary to a consultant at St. Bartholomew's and has her own flat nearby."

"What are her hobbies?" Rebecca asked. "Come on tell all."

"Well apart from Arsenal football, she likes sewing and she is training to work in Aromatherapy. She hasn't a large family as she is an only child, and her parents are both only children. She has a Granny and that's about all. She is going to find our family a bit overwhelming, so we'll do it slowly."

"Well she can't be shy," Elizabeth laughed "or she would never cope with you. Now when are you going to bring her to meet us?"

"Caroline will come to our New Year party, if that's all right? And meet everyone then. She will be twenty-two in the New Year. The same day as Grandpa, and Charlotte Anne, January 5th. So you won't have any excuse for not sending a card. She is not a quiet little mouse, just the opposite; she is a friendly girl with a bubbly personality."

"She would have to have, or she couldn't put up with you," laughed Rebecca. "We will be delighted to meet her Nick, and so will the rest of the family. Let's hope we don't put her off. We are not exactly quiet and there are such a lot of us."

"She is looking forward to it" Nick laughed. "And she says I am very lucky to be part of a big family."

We stopped at the service station and John had a good look at the photograph.

"She'll do," he smiled.

We enjoyed the break, had a good meal and stretched our legs walking around the shops and using the facilities. Then we all climbed back and enjoyed the comfort of the bigger car, which Nick now insisted on driving.

We arrived in good time and were welcomed by John's parents. They were thrilled with all our news and wanted to hear all about 'Alice in Wonderland.'

We all went to the Parish Church for the morning service and then we were going out for Christmas lunch. When we arrived at 'The Upper Crust', as the restaurant was called, John's sister and family were there to enjoy the meal with us. It seemed strange not to have to prepare anything, but it was a lovely change and best of all there was no washing up. We were all going to John's sister's for tea and there was a lot of fun talking about the old days when John and Jean were little. They were very interested to hear about Caroline and there was much speculation about another wedding.

We had enjoyed our break and felt quite rested. Nick said he was driving us home, so John and I sat in the back and the girls shared the front seat. Elizabeth first, and after the halfway stop, Rebecca. We picked up Toffee and Fudge on the way home and they were overjoyed to see us. Pam said she and Derek had so enjoyed having them that they were going to look for a dog for themselves.

"Derek really enjoyed taking them for walks," she said, "and it has done him good to have the exercise. He swears he has lost weight, in spite of Christmas."

There was an enormous post waiting for us. I scrambled through it taking out late Christmas cards and family mail. The rest I put on John's desk.

"That will keep him going for some time," I thought.

Nick had a meal with us and then returned to his flat, but we would see him again in less than a week accompanied by Caroline.

My next job was to organise food for the family get-together as well as the church buffet we give in the New Year to say 'Thank You' to the folk who work so hard during the year. The Stewards, Flower Arrangers, Organist and Choir Master and those who run Youth Club, and leaders of the Uniformed Organisations.

I start by making lists and this year Elizabeth and Rebecca helped a lot. I was in the middle of lists when John came out of his study.

"What about this then," he said, thrusting a large piece of paper into my hand.

I read it and looked up at him with a big smile on my face.

"This is really something, isn't it?" I grinned. It was a letter from a Housing Society looking for land to build twelve bungalows in this area. What they were offering was to build us a church, if they could have the land around our present church. All we would have to pay was for demolition, and inside furnishing.

This would have to be discussed widely of course and John wisely rang Norman Branston, and invited him and Margery to lunch with the Circuit Treasurer and his wife. This was only a preliminary talk about possibilities, but it was quite exciting.

CHAPTER FIVE

All our children came for the family get-together on New Year's Day, as well as Mum and Dad and, of course, Caroline. Nick had certainly been correct in saying she had a bubbly personality. She soon made friends with everyone and made a great fuss of Toffee and Fudge. She also begged to hold baby Emma, and had bought a lovely gift for her, a pink soft baby blanket to snuggle up to. Emma loved it. For everyone else she had brought a huge box of Thorntons Luxury Chocolates to share, a very acceptable gift. She came into the kitchen and soon had a tea towel in her hand ready to help with the washing up.

Mum said, "Well, Nick certainly waited until the right girl came along, but he has chosen well. A complete contrast to quiet Vanessa, but both boys have the right girl for them. I couldn't be happier." I felt the same.

Charlotte Anne and Richard had enjoyed their Christmas, although Charlotte Anne said, "it seemed so strange."

"Well," I said, "this is what happens when the family grows up and spreads its wings." Then I looked at her happy face and thought "there is something different about my daughter, I wonder?"

We had arranged one of our enormous buffet meals. That way everyone could have as much or as little as they wanted, and there was plenty of choice. I had bought disposable plates and dishes so that all that was needed when people had finished was a large dustbin bag. The only thing I did insist on having was proper cups or mugs and glasses.

Mum got me in a corner and told me again how much they were enjoying 'Westerley'. She assured me that they were extremely happy.

"I have no responsibilities for anything except our morning coffee and afternoon tea. And even that is because I choose to provide it. We could perfectly well go down to the dining room and have it. But I like to make it and sometimes invite our friends in to share it, or we go to their rooms. Life is just perfect. We are so fortunate. There is only one thing I miss and that can't be helped."

"What's that?" I asked. "Anything I can do anything about?"

"No you can't" she smiled. "It's just that sometimes I would love to make a cake or some shortbread, nothing big, but it just can't be done. I did ask Matron one day if it were possible to make a cake for everyone's tea. But she explained that I couldn't use the kitchen, as residents were not allowed in there for safety reasons. Of course I do understand."

"Before you go back," I said "do some baking here and take it back with you."

"Of course," she smiled, "I'll make some shortbread and take it back to share with friends."

"Give some to Matron" I smiled. "She may change her mind and make an exception. Who can resist your shortbread?"

Then she smiled at me and said "Charlotte Anne?" and raised her eyes.

"I thought the same," I said, "but she will tell me when she is ready, if we are right."

But it was Vanessa who took me into a corner and whispered that if all went well there would be a brother or sister for little Emma in July. What a thrill.

John told the family about his exciting news about a new church and everyone was very interested. Richard particularly so, and said,

"Mind you look after that organ, it's quite a good one." Then he told us he was having organ lessons. He had always loved the organ, but had not had time with all his other studies to take it up. Now, although he was still working hard for further qualifications, he felt he could take on organ lessons. He was already a competent pianist and we were very glad for him. John assured him that the organ would be looked after, and installed in any new building we had.

"That organ was given nearly a hundred years ago by the man whose land the church was built on. There are still family connections in the church and they will be consulted about any changes." John assured him.

We had just gone up to bed when there was a knock at our door. It was Charlotte Anne, and Richard was just behind her.

"Can we come in for a minute?"

I grinned at her and opened the door wide.

"Come on in," I said. "No one will hear us in here."

"This won't take a minute," she smiled, "but we think I might be pregnant. Now please don't tell anyone else, it's far too early to be sure. Anything may happen, but if all goes as we hope it will be in September. No one else knows. Richard is telling his Mum and Dad, and everyone else can be told when we are more certain."

We both hugged her and Richard, and said how delighted we were.

"Goodness," John said when they had gone to their room. "Two babies in the summer. Can you cope?"

"Watch me" I smiled.

The family dispersed the next day except Mum and Dad who were staying for the week. The twins were a great help at the buffet for our church officers, and we told them they could both have their instruments before they went back to school. We will go to Duck, Son and Pinker tomorrow and choose a violin for Elizabeth and a flute for Rebecca. They were both very excited and gave us a big hug.

John then went to meet his Church Council to tell them about the offer he had received. Norman had advised him to seek information about demolition.

"You know, John, this chapel was built over a hundred years ago and the bricks will be worth a fortune. Don't allow any demolition firm to make off with them."

"Well, that is a long way off," John told him, "but thanks for the advice."

I wanted to buy the wool and start one of my shawls, but I would have to be very careful. The twins are very quick, and would know it wasn't for Vanessa, as she had Emma's. I would just have to knit when they were not around.

John met his Church Council and told them about the offer from the Housing Society. They were very excited about it.

Derek said "Well, that solves the arguments about whether to enlarge the church, or pull it down and start again."

"How much do you think we would have to raise, John?" asked one of the officers. John explained that the bricks would be worth quite a lot of money and that a firm re-furbishing The Docks were interested in buying them.

"The Circuit Stewards and I are looking into it and will keep you informed. Another source of income will be the sale of the pews." There was a deathly silence.

"I think people will expect to have them put into the new church," Derek said.
"Several people have spoken to me about it."

That was a shock for John. He had expected to have chairs, and thought the only problem would be the choice of colour.

"This will have to be discussed at the Annual Church Meeting," he said, "but it makes no sense to have the old pews installed. It would mean we would need another large room for a hall, and obviously put the costs up."

Derek asked John for a word when the meeting ended. Apparently, the pews in the church were solid oak, and had been paid for by a family who still had connections in the church. The family had asked the Stewards what would happen to the pews if the church was demolished, and were assured they would be stored carefully and re-installed.

"Oh dear, yet another problem" John sighed.

The girls and I went back to school in January and I had another surprise. Transition's teacher was not coming back. Her husband had been promoted and moved to Coventry to work at Head Office. Mrs. Jenner called me into her office and offered me the post of Form Mistress to Transition Form. I was stunned. I loved the girls and it was exactly the right age group for me. I would also be able to go on teaching my older girls, and helping them with arithmetic. I didn't have to think about it and knew John would be pleased. I accepted the post with great joy. Mrs. Jenner explained that I could start right away, as their present teacher wasn't coming back.

"I will tell the school at our next assembly, and I'm sure you will find that you are most welcome."

She came into the classroom with me, as my next lesson was geography with Transition Form. The girls all clapped when Mrs. Jenner told them that I was now their Form Mistress and there were smiles all round. I couldn't wait to tell John and the twins, as well as the rest of the family. John and the girls were delighted and we were chattering away as usual when John gave us all a surprise.

"Now your mum has a permanent and secure job, I think we can think about a real holiday in the summer. What would you think about a holiday in Austria?" I was speechless, but the girls were not.

"Whoopee," shouted Elizabeth

"Great," shouted Rebecca.

"Whereabouts in Austria?" I asked.

"Well I think the first thing to do is go and get some brochures from the travel agents." John suggested. "Then we can all have a look and decide where to go, and for how long."

"The girls will need passports" I reminded John, "and are ours up to date?" John said he had no idea but would look into it. John had to hurry his meal as usual, and left in rather a hurry to keep an appointment. The girls and I finished more leisurely and then cleared and washed up.

Elizabeth said "Homework first and then we can talk about Austria. Come on 'Becs." I gave her a stern look and they went off to do their homework. We have provided them both with desks in their own rooms, but they often do it together, the dogs curled up at their feet, especially as they obviously have the same homework. They rarely asked for help and seemed to be coping with the more difficult subjects quite well. It was quite obvious that Elizabeth was more interested in the science side and Rebecca preferred the literature and language subjects. They both loved English, music, drama and literature. Rebecca's favourite language was Latin and she told us that when she was older she would love to learn Greek.

Their best friends were still Katie and Sammy, but they had quite a few other friends in their form, and some from other forms who were in drama group, choir or orchestra. It was good to know they were so happy.

Next day I was welcomed into the school as Form Mistress to Transition Form and the older girls were told that those who needed it would still have my help with arithmetic. I may also have time to help with R.E. I would certainly never be bored. When we arrived home from school we found John in the kitchen looking at holiday brochures.

After a drink and biscuits we all joined him and the girls said together, "Dad, what about Switzerland?"

"No," John told them, "it's far too expensive. Stick to Austria please. We will have to decide whether we go to the Mountains or the Lakes. We could, of course take the option of a double choice."

We all loved that idea. John said "Another option is for me to lead a party, take some of our church family and that would make it a lot cheaper."

"Stop right there," I interrupted. "I simply will not agree to that."

"Why ever not?" asked a startled John.

"Because you need a holiday as much as we do. Leading a group would mean you, were still on duty. No absolutely not." The girls agreed with me.

"We want you to be our Dad please. Just for once, we don't want to share you." John smiled and agreed.

"It was just a thought," he grinned.

We looked through the brochures again, but we all agreed that a holiday based in Innsbruck with an optional day in Salzburg would be the best choice for us. We would start saving up and go as soon as school broke up in early July. We would be home again before the excitement of new babies demanded our attention.

We had a very interesting morning in Gloucester. First we went to Thomas Cook the travel agents and booked our wonderful holiday. Then we had passport photographs taken of the twins. We had to laugh at the sad looking faces, but they would do. Then John took us all for coffee and cakes before going to the music shop to look at instruments.

The shop assistants were most helpful and different ones came to show us violins and flutes. They were obviously skilled assistants, and were most helpful. Rebecca chose her flute first, with a great deal of fun, as she blew too hard and caused a dog, which was with another customer, to throw back his head and really howl. The assistant explained that she was not blowing her recorder, and explained some of the techniques, needed for the flute. She also offered names of people who would give lessons, but Rebecca explained that she was at the Cathedral School, and they had specialist teachers who came in for music lessons.

Then Elizabeth asked about a violin.

The assistant said, "Just a moment," and disappeared. Then the manager came up to us and said, "I don't know if you would be interested, but we have a very good second-hand violin. It belonged to a professional violinist. In fact he was in the Halle Orchestra for many years. He recently died and his daughter brought the violin in saying he would want it to be played, not just put away in a cupboard. He had been a very small man so his violin was not a full size one."

Elizabeth said she would love to try it, so it was brought from the back room. It was obviously a very good one and had a beautiful tone.

John took me aside and whispered. "We could never afford it."

Of course Elizabeth loved it. It was just right for her and she was able to play a simple tune.

John said, "Dare I ask the price?"

"Well," the manager said, "when we acquired the violin there was a stipulation. The previous owner's daughter said she couldn't make a profit out of her father's violin. She asked us to find the right buyer for it, and she would give us a fee for selling it. But she wanted to know where it was going. Seeing you are a clergyman I think she might approve of this young lady. I'll give you her details and perhaps you will contact her. Here is her telephone number. Please give me a ring when you have come to a decision."

Elizabeth reluctantly handed the violin over. She kissed it and said "Bye little violin, I hope to see you soon."

Then we paid for Rebecca's flute and left the shop feeling rather dazed.

John rang the number he had been given as soon as we arrived home. The lady sounded very pleased that we were interested in her Dad's violin, and asked us to take Elizabeth to meet her. She gave us her address in Denmark Road and we arranged to take Elizabeth to see her in two days' time. She was a very nice lady and told us quite a lot about her Father.

"He loved his music," she said, "and was a very gifted violinist. I could not possibly sell his violin, yet it must be used by the right person." She obviously approved of Elizabeth and said she would be delighted for her to have it.

"You must promise me to take the greatest care of it and never to sell it," she said wiping her eyes. The violin obviously meant a lot to her.

Elizabeth asked her if she had a photograph of her father playing the violin.

"Oh yes," she smiled, "just a moment." Then she disappeared upstairs. She came down with a framed photograph of her father playing in the Halle Orchestra. He was indeed a small man; he had a lovely face and reminded me of my Dad. Elizabeth asked his name and was told he was William Stanley Greenwood.

"That is strange," Elizabeth said, "one of my Grandfathers is William, and the other one is Stanley."

"I think you were meant to have this don't you?" Miss Greenwood smiled.

"I would take the greatest care of it" Elizabeth assured her.

John then stepped in and said. "I can quite understand that you cannot sell your father's precious violin, but are you suggesting that Elizabeth can borrow it?"

"Oh no, not at all. As long as I have the assurance that it will be loved and cared for I am happy to give it to your daughter." We were staggered.

"What would you feel about us giving a donation to your favourite charity?" John asked.

"Haven't you got a building scheme for your church?" she asked. "I seem to have heard something about your Talent Scheme."

"Yes," John answered. "Do you think your Father would be happy about us giving a sum to the fund in his memory?"

"Nothing would please me more," she smiled. "I'm going to write a note to Duck, Son and Pinker, and instruct them to hand it over to Elizabeth after they have made sure it is tuned and in good order."

Then Elizabeth surprised us by asking. "Please could I have a copy of this photograph? I would look at it whenever I practised." Miss Greenwood assured Elizabeth that she could take the photograph now if she liked it.

"I have plenty more of Dad playing his violin" she smiled.

We left feeling extremely happy and told Miss Greenwood we would keep in touch, and let her know how Elizabeth was progressing. She seemed very pleased.

As we left she said "I have been praying for the right person to come along and I'm sure Dad had something to do with it."

Then she said to John "I don't believe in spirit people, but I have felt Dad's presence very much whilst you have been here. Do you think I'm being fanciful?"

"No, I don't" John assured her. "Many people feel their loved ones around them and why not?"

Then we left, looking forward to collecting the violin as soon as possible.

CHAPTER SIX

The next excitement was when we received a telephone call from Duck, Son and Pinker. They had refurbished the violin and had it tuned. It was in good order and they wondered when we could pick it up. Elizabeth was ecstatic and jumped up and down saying

"Can we go right away?" I waved my arm at her whilst holding the telephone with the other.

"We can be there in half-an-hour," I assured him. Elizabeth and Rebecca flew to collect coats and put on outdoor shoes. They were ready before I was. |John came in and looked surprised at all the bustle.

"Now what?" he asked.

"A call from Duck, Son and Pinker" I explained. "We can pick up the violin."

"Just give me a minute and I'll take you," he smiled.

We were there in less than half-an-hour and Elizabeth received her violin in its case.

"Can I just have a quick look?" she asked.

"You can, and you may." I gave her a look.

"Really Elizabeth." She grinned back and cheekily said

"Stop being school-marmish, just be Mum." Then she opened the case and carefully lifted her violin out. She noticed that the bow had been re-strung. Then putting it under her chin she played a scale and a simple tune. She looked so happy and so did Rebecca. John insisted on paying for the refurbishment, although we were told that Miss Greenwood had already paid it.

"Send it back to her" John grinned. "She has already been most generous." Then we went home and after tea the girls gave us a simple recital.

John left for his meeting with the Church Council. I knew this was the meeting where they would talk about the new Church, and how to re-furbish it. The question of chairs would have to be thrashed out before bringing the matter to the whole Church membership.

I got down to planning my lessons, and was surprised by a visit from Pam. She was looking very distressed and all she said was

"Can I come in and talk to you?" I gave her a hug and took her into the lounge.

"You know we have just come back from visiting our daughter in Bristol don't you?"

"Well yes, is everything all right?"

"No, it isn't" she said and promptly burst into tears.

"Let me put the kettle on, and then you can tell me all about it." I went into the kitchen, but Rebecca was there with the kettle already boiling.

"I saw Auntie Pam looking upset," she said, "I knew you would make her a cup of tea."

"Good girl" I said. My youngest two were certainly growing up. I took tea and gingerbread into the lounge and found Elizabeth in there comforting Pam. I waved them off to finish their homework, but Pam said.

"Oh please let them stay, it will save you having to explain."

"Well if you wish, but they would only know what is wrong if you wanted them to know."

"I know that very well, and it is quite O.K. Let them stay. It's my new granddaughter, little Millie. She's just not thriving."

"But I thought she was a lovely little baby when I saw her just a few weeks ago. What's happened?"

"You are quite right Anne, she is a beautiful baby, and until she started on solids there wasn't a problem. She is three months old now and just beginning to take solids. When I was feeding her she took her food all right, and seemed to enjoy it. Then, before she had finished she just threw it all up, and I mean threw it. It went right across the room in a big arc. I have fed many babies and I know they are all sick at times but this was quite different. I called her Mum and she said."

"Oh, not again."

"Sarah cleared it up, and I asked her how many times this had happened.

"Oh every time she eats anything. That's why I asked you to feed her. I thought I was doing something wrong." Then she broke down and cried. "They told me off at the clinic because Millie hadn't gained since the last time she was weighed. She is all right as long as she just drinks. She always seems thirsty, but as soon as she has anything to eat she brings it back."

"I fetched Derek," said Pam. "He agreed that we should ring the doctor. An appointment was fixed, but we had to come home, so Derek could attend the meeting next door. Sarah rang me this afternoon and said she had just got back from the surgery. The doctor wasn't sure what the problem was but he suspected it was something to do with amino acids. He referred her to Southmead Hospital to see a lady there who specialises in these rare conditions. I feel I must go with her and I shall stay until we find out what is wrong with our precious granddaughter. Is that all right?"

"Of course it is." I said. "Go right away and forget about us."

"We'll help Mum with the housework" the girls said together.

"You will keep in touch and let us know what is happening won't you?"

"Of course," Pam assured, me wiping her eyes. She looked a little better after her refreshment.

"Is Derek going to stay with you?"

"Yes, he is, and he surprised me by saying he would come to the hospital with us. You know how he hates such places. It shows how much he loves little Millie, that he wants to be there to hear what they have to say."

Pam stayed with us for the evening until John and Derek came in together from the meeting. Apparently it had gone very well. All the Church Council members could understand the nonsense of putting pews back into a new church, but didn't know how to appease the family whose ancestors had given the pews.

John told them to leave it to him. He would go and see the family and explain the position.

Derek then told us how worried they were about little Millie and this was, of course, news to John.

"You get off to Bristol and stay as long as you are needed," he said. "Don't worry about anything here." I think they left feeling a little easier, but of course very anxious.

"Mum, what exactly are 'amino acids'?" asked Elizabeth.

"I have no idea, except that they help us digest our food," I said.

"I'll ask our biology teacher tomorrow" she said. "Mr. Richards is sure to know."

It was now well after their bed time so I asked the girls about their homework. "All done" they assured me. "It was easy."

I shooed them off to bed and looked at my lessons for the next day. Maths, and history, with Transition. After that, time with my older girls. In the afternoon Transition had science and drama, so I was free, and would probably be asked to do some R.E. in the Senior School.

We hadn't been home long the next afternoon when John came in looking very pleased with himself.

"The question of chairs isn't going to be a problem," he smiled. "I've been to see Mrs. Daniels, the matriarch of the family. At first she was understandably upset at the very thought of chairs re-placing the pews."

"How on earth did you change her mind?" I asked. "Everyone I know of says she would never agree."

"Well I told her I understood her reluctance." Then I explained that a hundred years ago her family had given a wonderful gift to the church, which was appropriate for the time.

"What do you think they would do now?" I asked. "Just think about the restrictions. The only use for the pews would be on Sundays. We would also have to build another room for all activities, and chairs are the only answer. We would need to move them about for different occasions and only have them in rows for services or meetings. What do you think your family would do now?" She is a very intelligent woman and she didn't have to think for very long.

"John," she smiled, "You're quite right. Of course we must have chairs, but what will happen to the pews. I couldn't bear to see them destroyed."

"Good Heavens" I assured her. "They are very valuable and will be sold. The money we get from them will more than pay for the chairs."

"So my family would still provide the seating? I love that idea."

What a relief. The last thing John wanted was to upset anybody. "Now what about your brother and sisters, and your children?" John wanted to know.

"Leave them to me," she smiled. John was more than happy to do so.

John rang the Church Stewards; including Derek at his daughter's house.

"You'd charm the birds from the bushes," Derek said. "Well done."

"I'll make sure the Daniels family have a say in choosing the chairs." John said. "That is their right."

The next post brought the girls' passports. They were very thrilled, and said they felt very grown up. Indeed, they were growing up in every way, and were developing their own personalities and gifts. They were both doing well with their music, and were members of the school orchestra. They also loved their speech and drama lessons, and were entered as a form for the Cheltenham Festival. They had a girl in their form that had a speech defect, and they wondered if she would be allowed to enter with them. Sarah had been born with a harelip and cleft palate, and although she kept up with the rest in lessons, she didn't speak quite so clearly. Mrs. Hazelbury didn't like the thought of leaving her out of the group for 'Choral Speaking' and she took the opportunity to talk to the girls when Sarah was absent one day. One and all wanted to include her, so she took her place with the rest when the great day came.

The Festival was held in the Town Hall in Cheltenham and great was the excitement, both at home and at school. Imagine the delight when they came back to school with the cup. It was a great honour for their school, and everyone was delighted. Elizabeth asked Sarah how she managed some of the difficult words. Sarah laughed and said,

"If I know I can't pronounce it I just mime that bit, it's quite easy." Then they all laughed with her. Sarah is a lovely girl and extremely gifted at gymnastics, especially the trampoline. She has helped Rebecca a lot, and suggested she join the private club that she attends 'The Gloucester Springers."

We will have to think about. It would mean another night out, and of course, more expense. There are limits to both time and money, but we agree that Rebecca is exceptionally good on the trampoline. If we can manage it, we will.

CHAPTER SEVEN

A few days later we had a telephone call from Pam. The specialist at Southmead Hospital had thoroughly examined Millie.

"She even spent time watching her being fed," she said. "Of course the inevitable happened, and she immediately understood our concerns." She said she wanted to do some tests, before giving her diagnosis, but she was pretty certain that Millie had a very rare condition called Cystinosis.

Not one of us had heard of the condition.

"I'm not surprised" she smiled. "Very few people have heard of it. Only one, in two hundred thousand people worldwide suffers from it." Sarah burst into tears and her husband tried to comfort her.

"What have we done wrong"? He asked.

"Nothing, except marrying each other" was the astonishing reply.

"Let me explain as far as I am able," she said. "Very few people carry the gene for this condition, and most people would never know they did. But, if they marry someone who also carries the gene, then it may be passed on to their child."

"Does it mean that Sarah and I both have this gene then?" David asked.

"If that is what is wrong with Millie, 'yes' is the answer to your question."

We were all a bit stunned, but it was Derek who asked

"What do we do to help Millie? Is there a cure?"

"If that is what is wrong, then no. There is no known cure." This was shocking news, of course.

"But what will happen?" Her Daddy asked, "Surely if she can't take food she will die?" He took the baby in his arms and burying his face in her neck he kissed her, and said, "We all love her so much."

"No, your precious baby may well live well into adult life, but she will have to be fed through her tummy. If I am right about her diagnosis, then you will be shown how to care for her. Just remember that I may be wrong. Let us all hope so. If I am right then she will be under our care for the rest of her life."

"What happens now?" Sarah asked.

"I am going to ask you for blood tests, and will take Millie's. Then we will go from there."

Then Derek amazed everyone by saying "If blood transfusions are needed, or any sort of transplant, please let it be from me."

We were all stunned. After all this was Derek speaking. He faints at the sight of blood. Yet he was prepared to do all this for Millie.

"We thanked the Consultant and left with our precious baby. On the way home David said.

"I really trust that lady, but I still want another opinion. I am going to make an appointment at Great Ormond Street Hospital. In my opinion it is the best Children's Hospital in the world." We all agreed to back him up.

Little Millie was oblivious to all the upset and slept peacefully all the way home. Sarah had been given instructions on feeding her baby and we would see what happened when the diagnosis was either confirmed or rejected.

"Derek and I feel we can come home now, there is nothing more we can do, until they hear from the hospital."

"We'll be glad to see you both," I assured her "and we will all pray for little Millie. John has already put you on the 'prayer list' and the church folk are very concerned for you all."

Our girls were doing very well at school, both in lessons and all their activities. Rebecca absolutely loved her trampoline lessons and her gym teacher said she was exceptional. "When she has learned a few more skills I think she should enter for competitions." Rebecca was thrilled about this.

"Do you think there is any chance of a trampoline in the garden?" she asked.

"Perhaps, if we all club together for your next birthday. We'll just have to see." Elizabeth was just as thrilled with her violin and her teacher was very pleased with her. John had put a generous sum in an envelope and told Derek it was an anonymous gift for the Building Fund.

'In memory of a great musician, William Stanley Greenwood.'

He also took the opportunity to ask Derek about his problem. Whilst he was talking to Derek, he had had to break off twice to visit the toilet.

"You ought to get that checked," John told him after his second visit.

"Not on your Nellie," Derek answered him. "I've had more than enough of hospitals with Millie."

"But Derek, that's exactly why you should be checked right away. That baby is going to need her grandparents, very much. You know, even if it is prostate cancer it can be cured in the early stages. I've known many men, some in this church in fact, who have been cured in the early stages. Leave it too long, and it doesn't wait for your permission to get beyond help. You're not being fair to your family."

Derek was stunned. He sat down and pleaded with John for help.

"I'm simply scared stiff of operations and anything to do with hospitals," he admitted. John smiled at him and said.

"Millie is going to have to be brave, and she certainly needs you to be there for her, so do the rest of the family. Would you like me to come with you?"

That is how John came to visit first the doctor, and then Cheltenham Oncology Unit with Derek. In the end Derek was told he did indeed have prostate cancer, but that as it was in the very early stages, there was nothing to worry about. He was given choices for treatment and told to go home and talk it over with his wife. Pam was very grateful to John.

"He would never have gone without your chat," she said. "He told me you were pretty brutal and gave him no choice. But he valued your support very much."

Derek had been given three choices for treatment. None of them nice, but at least he had a choice. He could have an operation, or chemotherapy or radiotherapy.

He asked John if he and Pam could come and talk over the options with the two of us. We looked in our diaries and agreed on a date and time. There was not much discussion needed. Derek said.

"I just want the horrid thing out, but I don't mind admitting that I'm scared stiff."

John said, "I can't give you names of people who have gone through this and got rid of what you call the 'horrid thing.' I would be breaking a confidence, but would you mind if I talk to them and ask them to tell you of their experience?"

"John," he said, "I would trust you with anything. It would be good to talk to someone who has gone through this and come out the other side."

Then they told us the latest news about Millie. They had taken her up to Great Ormond Street and seen a world specialist on this rare condition. He explained the effects of the condition and that it could affect eyes and kidneys. He also gave them the address of people who ran 'The Cystinosis Foundation.' They will keep you in touch with other families and all medical advances. It is well worth supporting them, even if Millie turns out to have a different condition. Then he surprised them.

"Tell me why you have come all this way to see me, when you have the best specialist in the country on your doorstep?" Then he gave them the name of the lady they had seen at Southmead. That satisfied them.

He said, "Now we are just waiting to get the results of all the tests."

They went home happier than when they came and so were we.

Easter was not far off, although it was late this year. John thought we should make a long day of Easter Sunday. He suggested to his Church Council that there should be an 8 o'clock communion followed by Easter breakfast. The usual 10.30am service and then in the afternoon an Easter egg hunt in the Manse garden. In the evening he suggested a 'Songs of Praise' to end the day.

The Church Council agreed all this, and in the end the 'Songs of Praise' became a Circuit affair. Everyone enjoyed the whole day.

It ended for us with a very happy telephone call from Charlotte Anne telling us that her pregnancy had been confirmed, and that her baby was due in late September. I thought the twins would be ecstatic. They were of course, but surprised us by saying

"Oh we've known that for ages. We wondered when you would tell us."

Is it any wonder that we have to be very careful when we carry someone's secret?

Now I could knit in peace. I had already started on baby clothes for Emma's brother or sister. Now I could knit my shawl, even when the girls were around.

Charlotte Anne wanted to go on working as long as she could. We had told her that we would buy the pram, but there is always a lot of expense when a first baby is on the way. She felt very well, and her morning sickness had ended, so she saw no reason not to go on working as long as possible. Probably until the end of July she thought.

Richard was thoroughly enjoying his work, and he had his preaching and organ lessons as well. He was very thrilled about the baby and suggested they should get a holiday in as soon as possible. They rather thought they would like the Minehead area. They love all the Exmoor villages and they would take Mum and Dad out quite a bit.

They are going to try for the end of May. If they do, we will probably try to have a day in half term with them.

John was very busy with various meetings about the new Church. The pews have been sold to a charity that is building a church in a remote part of Africa. They are willing to wait until our church is demolished. The money they have offered will just about cover the cost of the chairs we will need. The Daniels family are delighted to think that their ancestors' pews will still be used in a church. The bricks are going to be used in the Docks refurbishment. All this will help with the cost of refurbishing our new church.

The actual building will be done by the Housing Association, using our land. It is all fitting together very well.

John thought there would be a problem when Mrs. Daniels asked him to call on her. However when he returned, he was smiling.

Mrs. Daniels whose name, by the way, is Mary, is well on in her eighties and thinking about her future. She wondered if she would qualify to have one of the houses being built on church land. John put her in touch with the Housing Society and she seemed very pleased.

"I would love to have a little house built on church land," she said.

Derek rang to say he had received a letter from Cheltenham Hospital. They would admit him to the Oncology Ward in ten days. He would be admitted in the morning and have his operation later in the day. He was given instructions and Pam would see he stuck to them. John told him he would take them both, see Derek was admitted and call later to bring Pam home. I asked if she would like to come here, but she said she would rather be at home.

"The family will be ringing me and I will be perfectly all right," she said. In fact it was all over before anyone started getting worried. There had been a cancellation, and as Derek was all prepared he was taken to theatre much earlier than anyone expected. Pam rang us just as we arrived home from school and said.

"It's all over and Derek is back on the ward. I can go in and see him tonight." Dear Ted had offered to take her, and John said he would call in later.

John came home about 7 o'clock, very happy and surprised that Derek was able to talk to him as though nothing had happened. Derek told him that he hadn't felt a thing and had certainly seen no blood. When John was telling us he laughed and said.

"You know I think Derek expected to be strapped down and dealt with like they did in the days before anaesthetics. He was surprised to wake up and find it was all over. He will soon be home and able to give his mind to Millie and her troubles."

CHAPTER EIGHT

Half term seemed to come very quickly. John had arranged to take a day off and we agreed to meet Charlotte Anne and Richard at 'Westerley.' After a cup of coffee with Mum and Dad we were all going off for a trip around our favourite villages. We had two cars of course, and as we had Toffee and Fudge with us we needed them both. The twins and their dogs were going with Charlotte Anne and Richard. Mum and Dad settled comfortably in the back of ours. We set off first for a trip to the top of North Hill where we wandered around amongst the beautiful rhododendrons. The gorse was also in bloom of course, and the girls ran races with Toffee and Fudge. There was no contest, the dogs always won.

We sat admiring the beautiful North Devon cliffs and watched the birds. What a variety there were. Buzzards quartered the sky, competing with the various gulls, but there were other birds of prey. We could have done with Nick to identify them. Certainly there were kestrels, but there were others, and no one was sure of them. We thought there were hen harriers, and Rebecca said there were sparrow hawks, but no one was quite sure.

The little birds on the hedges were easier to identify. The chaffinches were almost tame, and came very close to pick up biscuit crumbs we threw for them. A group of goldfinches were enjoying the bounty from the gorse bushes and thistles. John said he could hear larks, and driving away we did see some, rising up in song.

The next stop was Selworthy. We parked the cars and admired the view from the church doorway. It was a beautiful clear day and we could see Dunkery Beacon in the distance. We wandered around the beautiful green and the dogs loved playing splash in the little stream. We decided to have lunch in the tea-room on the green and then drive on to Porlock. We spent quite a while in Porlock itself and then noticed that Mum and Dad were looking tired.

Richard said he would take his passengers over the toll road into Lynmouth. We were quite happy to take Mum and Dad back to 'Westerley'. They had thoroughly enjoyed their day, but admitted to feeling they had had enough. I yawned and gave myself quite a jolt. I was feeling like a cup of tea and a rest. Surely John and I were not getting old? Then I laughed for we were, after all, grandparents to Emma, with two more on the way.

We waved the youngsters off, and climbed back in our car heading for 'Westerley'. When we arrived in Mum and Dad's room I put the kettle on and we sat looking up at the slopes of North Hill. As we sat enjoying our tea and shortbread I asked Mum where the shortbread had come from?

"It tastes like yours," I said.

"Well that is very re-assuring" Mum laughed. "Of course it's mine."

"But how did you manage that then?" I asked.

"Well," Mum laughed, "it was your idea. When we got back after Christmas, I did as you suggested and gave Matron a piece of shortbread when she came in for a cup of tea."

"This is your handwork, isn't it?" she asked. I assured her it was and she looked very thoughtful.

"I can't allow you to use the kitchen," she said, "but what about using my private kitchen? We are having a coffee morning, as you know, in February. Would you like to use my kitchen and make some to sell?"

"I did just that, and not only shortbread, I offered to bake some scones as well. Now, if I feel like it, I only have to ask, and I am allowed to use the kitchen. The only proviso is that I leave the kitchen clean and tidy. And I would certainly do that anyway. The residents enjoy my bounty with their cup of afternoon tea, and they always recognise it as mine."

"Oh! Lottie has been busy again," they smile.

Dad is happy, still preaching and enjoys using 'The Preachers' Room' to prepare his services. He keeps talking about giving up, but the chapels in the area still look forward to his services so he keeps going. He talked to John about it, and explained that all his services were in the village chapels around Minehead. The congregations were all elderly folk and they liked the old hymns and his sort of sermons.

"The younger preachers all want these modern services with new hymns, They say my services suit them better, so I keep going."

We enjoyed our quiet chat with Mum and Dad in their comfortable room and had our evening meal with them.

Charlotte Anne and Richard arrived with the twins and dogs about 7 o'clock and we began to think about going home. Charlotte Anne, I noticed, had quite a nice little bump for someone only five months pregnant. She certainly looked very well and they were both looking forward to being parents. She showed me some very pretty baby clothes they had bought in Lynmouth, and Mum showed her what she was knitting. It was a small blanket to put on a pushchair or car seat.

"I'm doing one each for you and Vanessa," she said. Mum loves her magazine called 'People's Friend' and she had seen the pattern in the magazine soon after getting home after Christmas. She was knitting a pale blue one for Vanessa and a pretty lemon one for Charlotte Anne, who was thrilled with it, especially as Mum said

"I chose a wool that could be washed in the washing machine."

It was time to go, and Charlotte Anne and Richard left just before us. As they left Mum said, with a twinkle in her eye, "I think I had better knit two blankets for Charlotte Anne."

We all gave Mum and Dad a big hug as we left and Toffee and Fudge enjoyed their pats. Then we left, promising to fetch them for a break in the summer holidays.

"I'll ring as soon as we get home," I called from the car. We left them standing together looking very happy.

We had a good journey back, stopping at a service station to give the dogs a run and stretch our legs. We arrived home to find the usual pile of post and the answer phone full of messages. Elizabeth said she would ring Nana and let them know we were back. Rebecca took the dogs into the garden. John went into the study to deal with his post and I organised a drink for everyone. I was just in the middle of this when I heard the telephone ring. Immediately John came into the kitchen looking dreadful.

"It's your Dad love, come here." He gave me a big hug and then led me into the study. The girls were behind us looking very worried.

I picked up the telephone and said, "Dad, whatever is it?"

"Mum's gone," he said blankly.

"Gone where?" I asked stupidly.

"You had only been gone for about half-an-hour" Dad said. "We sat down and talked about our happy day. Then your Mum said.

"Look after them all, I'll never see these new babies."

"Then she sat back and fell asleep. I nodded off and when I woke up I could see something was wrong. I rang Matron, who came immediately."

"I'm sorry," she said, Lottie has gone."

"Then she led me out and sat me down in another room and brought me a cup of tea. I never drank it. I just wanted to ring you and the boys. Whatever am I going to do?" Then he burst into tears.

Before I could say anything to him Matron picked up the telephone and explained more to me.

"I'm taking your Dad into their friend next door and they will look after him." Then she explained that she must send for a doctor and get the Funeral Director to come.

I told her that I would ring my brothers and then be with Dad as soon as possible. Then I told her. "Charlotte Anne and Richard are very close, in a Boarding House in the next road. They will be Dad's best comfort just now."

John took the telephone from me and sat me down on the settee. The twins sat one on each side of me with their arms around me.

"Let me organise this" he said. He thanked Matron for her help and then explained that he would ring Charlotte Anne and Richard. They will come and take Dad away with them and look after him until we get there.

He found the address he wanted and rang the proprietors. He explained the position and they were very kind.

"Would your father-in-law like to come here and be with them? I have a single room vacant right next to them."

John thanked them, but said he just needed to talk to them.
"Bring Richard to the telephone please."
Poor Richard was quite shocked, but said he would tell Charlotte Anne the sad news and they would go straight back to 'Westerley.'

"We will stay with him until you get here," he said. So that is what happened.

The twins said they were quite old enough to stay by themselves, but if we liked they would ring someone and ask for help.

"Auntie Pam and Uncle Derek will come if you ask them," they said.

Elizabeth was already on the telephone and of course, Pam said she and Derek would be here as soon as possible. By this time it was 9 o'clock and John was looking at his diary for the next day. He was trying to sort out who would take his Women's Meeting and his other evening meeting when Pam and Derek arrived.

Derek went to John and said. "When we are in trouble you take over. Now you must let us help you. We will see to everything. All we need is for you to tell us what you had planned and we will do it, or get the appropriate person to do it for us. You just look after your family and we will do the rest."

Pam was comforting the girls, and the dogs were getting in everyone's way, wondering what was wrong. Pam put them in the garden and then made us all a drink. The one I had been making before that awful phone call was, of course, stone cold.

John went through his diary and also rang one of the other ministers who took over his communion service, and would see to the couple who were coming to arrange a wedding. Derek would do the rest.

John rang my brothers, who were of course, shocked. We arranged to meet at 'Westerley' the next day, to arrange everything.

It was nearly midnight when John and I arrived at 'Westerley'. What a change in only a few hours. Matron had kindly found another room for Dad and, of course, Charlotte Anne and Richard were with him.

We were shocked by the change in Dad. In only a few hours he looked at least ten years older. The doctor had been and said Mum had died very peacefully. Her heart had just stopped beating. The Funeral Director had been and taken her body to the chapel of rest, and just awaited our instructions. We all decided to wait for any further decisions until my brothers and their wives arrived.

Dad said, "We had discussed all this, of course. We both want cremation. We don't want you left with graves to look after. We just want everything to be as simple as possible. Certainly we will have a service of 'Thanksgiving for Life', not a funeral service. I wouldn't want her coffin carried about. The only hymn I would definitely choose is our family hymn. The only other thing we discussed is the waste of money on flowers. One family spray of flowers will be enough. If people want to give donations it must be for 'The National Children's Home'" Charlotte Anne was pleased about that.

When Rob and Eleanor arrived next morning they had Carey Jane with them. This was a lovely surprise and it gave Dad a lot of comfort to have his two older granddaughters with him.

"I never thought you could get time off from your studies" he said, giving her a big hug." She explained that she had asked for compassionate leave and received it. Soon after Chris and Lucy arrived.

People around were quite surprised to hear us laughing, but we knew Mum and Dad didn't want weeping. Of course, although we were upset, all of us knew that Mum was safe and probably having a wonderful time in heaven.

She never knew her own mother, for she had died in childbirth leaving three older children who were all under eight. Her father was a deep-sea fisherman and away at sea for long periods. The boys went to live with their father's sister in Leith and the two girls went to their Granny Webster who lived in Rochdale, with her two unmarried daughters, our great Aunties, Fie and Bella. Our Auntie Nellie was five years old and of course Mum was newly born.

We talked about Granny Webster, who Rob and I just remembered, and our Auntie Fie and Auntie Bella. There would be a great re-union and of course, Mum would meet her Mother for the first time.

Then we decided on a date for Mum's service after consulting with their minister. He kindly asked if Rob and John wanted to take part, but both declined. I knew I needed John beside me and Eleanor would want Rob. It was best for someone else to take the whole service.

We had no trouble choosing hymns and we decided that we would meet at the crematorium. Just family would be present and it would be very short. Then we would go to Mum and Dad's church for the service of 'Thanksgiving for her life'.

Rob and I talked about what was best for Dad. He said he would like to stay put in 'Westerley' until it was all over. Then he would love to come and stay for a while with each of us. I told him that if he wanted to make a permanent home with us he was very welcome. He said it was lovely to have the choice, but he would have to think about it.

We had arranged with Matron to have lunch at 'Westerley' and Dad wanted us ladies to go through Mum's things.

"Take anything you want and the rest can go to the Charity Shop."

We did all that whilst the men helped Dad sort his things out as he was moving to a single room.

We kept a few things of Mum's to give to her grandchildren. Dad had her wedding ring in his pocket. Looking very tearful he said.

"What am I supposed to do with this? She has worn it for nearly sixty years."

"Put it on my finger for now" I said. "And the next granddaughter to get married will be offered her Granny's ring. Will that do?"

He looked very pleased. Mum didn't have a lot of jewellery, but the one or two nice pieces we divided up between us. I chose two rather nice necklaces for the twins. They were semi-precious stones, but pretty, and I knew the girls would like them. Charlotte Anne chose a locket, which had a photograph of Granny Webster on one side and Auntie Bella and Auntie Fie on the other. She would treasure that.

Carey had another locket, which had a picture of Auntie Nellie aged about twelve and Mum aged about seven. Lucy chose a nice necklace with an enamel snowdrop on the end for Kate. The rest were given to Mum's friends. Mum had a lot of books and these we shared between us. Most of their belongings had been got rid of when they went in to 'Westerley.' Then I remembered Mum's baking stone. The one she used for her shortbread. That wasn't going anywhere. I asked Dad where it was, and he said he thought it was in Matron's kitchen. I would pick it up when we left.

John is chaplain to a geriatric hospital in Gloucester and said they would be glad of Mum's clothes.

Dad agreed and said. "I don't think I would like to see someone else wearing her clothes. If they go to the local charity shop I might see someone walking about in them. It would be a bit upsetting."

We bundled them all into a big bag and John put them in the boot of the car straight away. Dad told us that he was sure they both had life insurance to pay for the funeral.

Rob said, "Do you want to see to it, or would you like me to?"

Dad said, "Oh will you? I'd be most grateful if you will see to everything, I just don't feel up to coping with it all."

Chris said he would take on the business of writing to all the rest of the family and letting them know arrangements. Before we left we arranged that after Mum's service we would book a table at a local restaurant.

This was not necessary at all. In the end Mum's friends at her church decided they would put on a meal for everyone coming to the service. They let Dad know what was happening and said, " think no more about it, it's all arranged."

Dad was truly grateful. We left him with his friends, after seeing him comfortable in his new smaller room. He told us he was most grateful that Matron had only put one bed in his room. She had left Mum's bed for Dad and put his in store.

"Everyone has been so kind" Dad said. "What on earth do people do who have no close family? I could never have managed without you."

"You don't have to worry," we assured him. "You have all of us."

Then we left.

CHAPTER NINE

The service at the crematorium was very short. Only family and very close friends attended. There had been much discussion as to whether the younger grandchildren should come. In the end we left it to them and they all decided they wanted to be there. Vanessa's parents looked after Emma and her other great grandson was looked after by his Mum's best friend. Otherwise her whole family were present. Rob and Chris supported Dad on each side. Charlotte Anne and Richard said they would have Elizabeth and Rebecca between them, and I certainly needed to hold John's hand. The only other people present were Matron and two couples from 'Westerley,' and two or three close friends from church.

A spray of red roses lay along the coffin. Mum's minister conducted the service and then we all went back to her church for the service of 'Thanksgiving for her life.'

The night before I had experienced a most extraordinary dream. I had seen Mum in a beautiful garden surrounded by her relatives. There was Granny Webster, Auntie Fie, Auntie Bella and another lady who I knew must be her own Mother. She was very happy and she turned to look at me and said,

"Tell them all I am so happy and will wait for Bill to come to me. Just look after them all."

Then I woke up and knew what I had to do. We had all said we couldn't possibly take any part in the thanksgiving service, but I knew what I must do. I told John and he agreed with me.

I explained to George Martell, her minister and friend, what had happened and he said

"Come and tell everyone before I begin the service."

I fixed my eyes on John and simply told them about my dream. Then the service began with the hymn 'Morning has broken.'

The church is not large, but it was packed, and that helped the singing. George spoke about Mum in a lovely way, even making us laugh, when he described her gifts. He told us that Mum was certainly going to be missed, and assured us all that Dad would be well looked after. Then after a few prayers we sang our family hymn.

'O Thou who camest from above.' to the tune Hereford.

That did it. We were all crying, but it didn't matter. We were ushered into the schoolroom and a wonderful spread awaited us. A collection plate was put at the back and when we left we could see it was full. The treasurer sent Rob a cheque for over three hundred pounds, and explained that many of the people at the service were from churches all around Minehead, where Mum had been a 'speaker' at their Women's Meetings.

Dad was going home with Rob and Eleanor. Then Chris and Lucy were collecting him. They were keeping him until we came back from Austria. John had asked Dad if he would like to come with us. He thought about it and said

"No, but thanks for the offer. My wandering days are over and I don't think I could cope with that sort of holiday. I'll stay with the boys until you get back."

We arranged that Chris and Lucy would bring him to us when we were back at home.

The younger children said they were glad they had been part of it all.

"We wouldn't have missed it," our two said, although they both admitted to holding hands during the service at the crematorium.

We had asked that Mum's ashes be scattered amongst the roses. Her spray of roses from the family was taken back to 'Westerley' for them to enjoy.

In the end Rob was able to send a very nice cheque to The National Children's Home and they acknowledged it gratefully.

We were only back at school after the half term holiday for a few days when it was examination time.

Neither I, nor the girls were involved in the public examinations, but there were important end of year examinations to prepare for. The girls worked hard at revision and I wrote papers for Transition for English, mathematics, history, geography and R.E.

Most of Transition were hoping to go into the Senior School, if they reached the required standard. Some were hoping for a scholarship or bursary. Some had sat the entrance examinations for local grammar schools and already knew where they were going. One or two were hoping for places at Cheltenham Ladies' College or Marlborough High School. They all hoped to do well in these examinations and worked hard.

To keep the school quiet, whilst public examinations were taking place in the hall, our end of year examinations were taken in the form rooms at the same time. When the examination papers had been collected the girls were instructed to leave the rooms very quietly and go right into the grounds away from hall before they spoke.

This all meant different timetables. There was a lot more use of the playing fields, whilst inter-house matches took place. Another day, coaches took all non-examinees off to the Malvern Show. This gave all the girls involved in public examinations a quieter time.

Sports Day came at the end of term, when all examinations were over and was enjoyed by everyone. Our family were delighted when Plantagenet House won the sports cup having scored most points overall.

The pupils could relax a little over the last few weeks of term, although the staff, of course, had marking and reports to write.

I was very pleased with my form, but on the last day of term I wondered what they were up to. We all went into end of year Assembly and they sat very properly until they found the hymn. Then I could sense a few giggles and wondered what my little imps were up to. When it came to the last verse I knew. In the line

'The breadth, length, depth and height to prove' the whole form sang 'volume to prove', instead. We had struggled long and hard to understand what 'volume' meant, now I knew they would never forget it. I didn't tell them off, but gave them one of my 'looks'. Some of the staff had noticed and wanted to know what it was all about. We all had a good laugh.

Our own girls had done very well and were in the top five for everything except art. Neither being artistic. Rebecca came top in

French, and Elizabeth came top in science. Overall Elizabeth came third in the form and Rebecca fourth. If we ignored their art marks they would have been equal top, so we were very pleased with them and told them they deserved their holiday in Austria.

School finished on the Tuesday, and we were off to Austria on the following Friday for two weeks. We just had two full days to pack, organise the dogs and leave everything in order at home.

John had taken his three weeks holiday together, so he was supposed to be free to help. Of course if we are at home that never happens. People still wanted to see him and thought just a few minutes with them wouldn't matter.

The first one to call was young Benedick. He was just ready to go into the sixth form at the local grammar school. He had chosen his subjects and was all set for a career as a scientist. He had done very well in his '0' levels and had chosen maths, physics and chemistry for his 'A' level course.

John took him into the study and was with him for a long time. Then they both came into the kitchen smiling and John said.

"This young man feels he ought to study religious knowledge. I told him that it was your main course, and wondered if he felt he should teach science with religious knowledge."

"Tell Anne what you think about that, Benedick."

"No. I don't think that at all. I feel God would like me to be a minister."

This was a great surprise and I asked him why he was so sure.

"I have been struggling with maths, and wondered if I should ask for extra tuition. Then I felt I didn't really want that either. I didn't understand what was wrong with me, for I have wanted to be a scientist since I was little. I think The Ladybird book 'Light, Bulbs, and Batteries' started my interest. I was about seven then. I loved physics and chemistry and always did well in exams. I was all right with maths in the early years, but always struggled a bit after third year."

"Last Sunday John was preaching about his call to The Ministry, and I felt very emotional. I felt I wanted to be like him. Now I don't know what to do. So I thought I would come and talk to John about it."

"Well this is a surprise," I smiled at him. "And what did John have to say to you?" I asked.

John smiled and said, "I was not altogether surprised. You know Benedick has always read the lessons very well, and twice now he has read the prayers at the start of the service. People have commented about his ability and sincerity."

"Have you talked to your parents about this?" I asked.

"Yes. They knew I was in a strange mood last Sunday and I told them what I felt."

"Mum told me I must talk to John about this. "I know he is on holiday but give him a ring and see what he says."

"Do you feel any better for your talk with John?" I asked.

"Oh yes, I do, and he has given me some books to read. I feel more certain than ever that this is what I must do. It is still a shock, but I feel happier about it and I'll definitely take religious knowledge at 'A' level instead of maths. If I still feel it is right for me, John says he will tell me what steps to take. He is going to let me help him with services for a start. It's quite exciting."

Benedick left looking a lot happier, and John was still talking about it when the doorbell rang. It was Derek looking very worried.

"Oh John," he said, "I know you are officially on holiday, but Millie is going into hospital. All the tests prove that she has this condition called 'Cystinosis' and they are going to put tubes in to feed her through. I haven't told Pam yet. She is out shopping and I answered the phone. It was our daughter and she had just got the information. So she rang me. What on earth are we going to do?"

John put his arm around Derek and brought him into the kitchen where I was preparing lunch.

I put the kettle on and we sat down to try and calm Derek. Elizabeth came in and found us.

"We have put all our holiday clothes on our beds" she explained. "But we wondered whether we should travel in jeans or dresses."

"Whichever you like and would be most comfortable in," I answered. Then Elizabeth turned to Derek.

"Will you still be able to look after Toffee and Fudge?"

He assured her that they would, but told her they were putting off looking for a dog of their own until they were sure what Millie would need.

Rebecca came down to see what was taking her sister so long, and joined in the conversation.

"You don't need to put off having your own dog," she said, "You can always bring it here. If we are here, of course."

Derek thanked her and said he had better get home and wait for Pam.

"I must leave you folk in peace to get on with your holiday packing."

John was just showing him out when someone else arrived. It was a stranger, but someone wanting to arrange a wedding. John explained that we were on holiday, but he took her into the study and made a date for her to see him when we returned.

I went into the kitchen to check on the Chicken and Mango Pie and then to help Elizabeth and Rebecca with their packing.

I heard the telephone ringing and wondered why John wasn't answering it. I ran downstairs and found the study empty so I picked up the phone.

"Oh, I thought you must be out," said a weary voice I didn't recognise.

"Can you tell me what time the last bus goes into town? I can't find out and I didn't know who to ask."

"I have no idea," I answered. "Why don't you ring the bus station?"

John came in through the back door. A 'gentleman of the road' had knocked at the back door needing help. John gave him a drink and a sandwich and sent him on his way.

"As soon as we have had lunch," he said, "we are going out. We are supposed to be on holiday."

We all laughed and agreed.

Over lunch we discussed where to go for the afternoon, but were disturbed by yet another phone call. This time a helpful one.

One of our members asked how we were getting to Gatwick for our flight to Austria. John explained that we were going up the night before and staying for bed and breakfast. We can also leave our car there for the fortnight, and take an early morning taxi to the airport.

"Well I am just retired as you know," said our caller, "and I am quite free to take you to the airport however early, and pick you up again when you return."

This was indeed a wonderful help and John told Mike we would gladly accept his offer. People really are very kind and helpful.

We decided to take a trip into the Cotswolds, perhaps Burford or Bourton on the Water. It never happened. We had a frantic telephone call from Jane. Baby Beth was having a convulsion and she was very frightened. We all piled into the car and arrived before Jane had managed to ring the doctor. Little Beth was still convulsing and I took her from Jane put her on her tummy across my knee and patted her back. She coughed up a lot of nasty mucous and then lay back exhausted.

Jane rang the doctor and explained what had happened. He asked if she could bring the baby to the surgery and John nodded to her that he would take her. The twins were playing with Jonathan and Lucy trying to distract them.

John drove Jane and the baby to the doctor and I stayed with the rest. They were back before long and Jane was looking much better. The doctor explained that it was not at all unusual for babies with Downs Syndrome to have convulsions. He told her what to do if it happened again, and made an appointment at the hospital so she could be tested for epilepsy.

Jane insisted we stay for tea and we all enjoyed seeing Bethany splash happily in her bath. Our two had a lovely cuddle with their little goddaughter, and helped put her to bed.

On the way home John said. "Get all the packing finished tonight. Everyone up early tomorrow and we are off to the Cotswolds. No stopping for breakfast I'll treat us all at 'The Basket Maker.' They do lovely breakfasts."

We all leapt at the idea and so started our holiday a day earlier than expected.

CHAPTER TEN

Mike called for us at five thirty next morning. It was an easy drive at that time in the morning, and there was very little traffic on the motorway. We arrived at Gatwick before 9 o'clock and invited Mike to join us for a drink before he returned. He told us he would rather stop on the motorway for breakfast. We all thanked him and John offered petrol money. He refused saying.

"After all you do for us? No way." He checked again on our date and time of return from Austria and assured us he would be waiting for us in the arrival area. Then he left and we realised we were actually on holiday.

We checked our luggage in and went through Customs. Then we found somewhere to eat and knew we had an-hour-and a-half before we were due to fly to Innsbruck.

We had never been at an airport before and were quite interested in all that was going on. We hadn't realised what a large shopping centre it was and after checking on our flight, we enjoyed a rare shopping trip. We didn't buy much except magazines, and a few sweets for the journey, but we all enjoyed browsing in the bookshops.

Our flight was on time, and we were very excited as we boarded our plane. The girls had seats in front of ours and the plane was soon full. The family across the aisle from Elizabeth and Rebecca had two small children with them. A boy called Nathanael who was about three years old and a little girl about ten months old called Isabelle. Our two were very interested and were soon talking to them.

Taking off felt very strange. The plane ran along the runway at high speed and it felt as though the ground fell away from us. It was only when we looked out of the window and saw the ground beneath us that we realised we were airborne.

I loved the feeling, and thought how wonderful it would be to go on a really long flight. Our flight was less than two hours, but we all thoroughly enjoyed it.

When we taxied on to the runway at Innsbruck we all had to alter our watches and the first thing that struck us was how hot it was. We were soon stripping off cardigans.

A coach was waiting to take us to our hotel and the family with the children were obviously with our party. Nathanael took Elizabeth's hand and informed her he would sit with her on the coach. Rebecca smiled and held out her arms to Isabelle who smiled and came to her. Their mother said. "It looks as though my family have adopted your twins. Do you mind?"

"Only that I didn't get a look in" I grinned.

We all boarded the coach and were driven through the most amazing scenery to our hotel called 'The Tyrollerhof' on the outskirts of Innsbruck.

The owner of the hotel and his wife came on to the coach and welcomed us all with the Austrian greeting "Gruss Gott," which means 'God's Greeting'. We were shown into the lounge and our guide explained where our rooms were, and we were introduced to the staff. They made us very welcome, and told us about meal times, and the facilities in the hotel.

We were booked for bed and continental breakfast, which was buffet style. Then we were to have an evening meal at 6 30.pm. This was a three-course meal and there was a choice for each course. We knew we were all going to enjoy this holiday very much.

We were served with coffee in the lounge, whilst our guide explained that there were three all-day tours included in our holiday. We could book for extra ones if we felt inclined, but the rest of the day was free. We decided that we would like to go on the bus to Innsbruck and explore. According to the leaflets, which were distributed, there was a lot to see. Buses ran from outside the hotel every fifteen minutes and the guide explained where to get the bus back again.

We went to our adjoining rooms where we found our cases, which had been brought up in the lift by the porters whilst we were having coffee.

We were delighted with our double room, which was beautifully decorated in cream and maroon, with gold accessories. There was a shower room and toilet through a door between the wardrobes and here we found towels, face flannels and plenty of toiletries.

The girls' room next door had twin beds and was in pretty shades of blue. They were delighted with it, but were surprised by the huge square pillows.

We all washed and changed and then set off to explore Innsbruck. We had given the girls their pocket money in Austrian shillings and told them it had to last for the fortnight. They had also been saving up for this holiday, and we discovered that both sets of grandparents had given them a donation. John said we would pay all their expenses and they could choose their birthday present. Anything else must come from their own money, so they must be careful not to waste money on trivialities.

The bus came along quite soon, and deposited us at the bus station in the middle of the shopping centre.

What wonderful shops, and most of them had tables, with huge umbrellas all along the pavements. We went into one shop selling wooden toys. There was an amazing number, and all hand-made from wood. I bought four baby rattles, which were easy for small hands to hold and had a little bell hidden in the top, which would also make a good teething ring. A little leaflet with each one said they were perfectly safe to chew on. Of course these were written in German, but there were several translations, luckily one in English. They were marked at a reasonable price; about five pounds each in our money. They would do for our new grandchildren and the spare ones would do for presents.

We were surprised, and very thankful that many of the Austrians could speak English. Rebecca said she loved the sound of German and was looking forward to learning the language next year. Elizabeth turned her nose up.

"Not for me thank you. French is bad enough."

One of the shops was a large department store and we wandered about, interested in the differences from our own large stores. It was a bit like Harrods I thought.

The prices were a problem. Marked in shillings they looked astronomical enough anyway. We could tell by the price of ordinary things like handkerchiefs that they were way above our prices. One man's handkerchief would be about five pounds in our money. We would certainly have to be careful with our present buying. However we did buy little Emma an Austrian dress. It was pale pink with a white blouse and fancy apron. She would look adorable in it.

We had a light lunch in one of the outside cafés and then wandered off to look at the Cathedral. The organist was playing Bach's Toccata and Fugue in D Minor, and we all sat down to listen. Then John said we should find the famous Golden Roof. It was only a small roof over a balcony, but with the sun shining on it, it was very impressive. Then we wandered down to look at 'The Inn', the river on which the city was built and named.

We noticed that the houses built on the other side of the Inn, matched the shape of the mountains behind them. Very clever.

It was time to look for afternoon tea and we had a drink and a cake at one of the cafés facing the river. Elizabeth suddenly gave a squawk and nearly spilled her milk shake.

"Dad," she said, "I've just had an idea. Elinor Brent-Dyer wrote her Chalet School books about this area. I'm sure she mentions Innsbruck in the very first book. The girls came to Innsbruck station and then went next day to Tiernsee. I looked it all up in my atlas at school, and it's really called Pertisau. The lake she called Tiernsee is really Lake Achensee."

"That's right" put in Rebecca, "oh please, please can we go?"

"Your Mum and I have already talked about this. We thought you could have an early birthday treat here. So if you both want to go to Lake Achensee we certainly can and what is more we may," John said with a grin. It was lost on them.

The girls hugged each other before giving us a hug.

"Oh what a treat," they said together. Elizabeth then told us that she had brought the first two books in the series to read again and try to identify the places mentioned in the books.

"When can we go?" they asked together.

"When we get back to the hotel we will sit down and look at what is planned. Then we can choose a suitable day to go. Will that do?" I asked. They both nodded and sat back satisfied.

Then we went for a walk through the beautiful grounds of the Imperial Palace. We caught the bus back to our hotel and just had time to have a wash and tidy ourselves before going down to dinner.

There was a huge choice and the waitresses kindly explained the dishes. They were quite different from our usual meals, but very tasty and we all enjoyed them. In the evening we went for a short walk and met again the family with the two children. They had been to the park and were just returning to put the children to bed when we met them. Nathanael grabbed Elizabeth's hand and asked if she would come and read his bedtime story. Elizabeth looked at his Mummy and she said.

"Only if you want to, you must not let Nathanael decide. He has been talking about you all day."

Elizabeth laughed and assured Val, as we had been told to call her that she would love to read to the little boy. Then Val turned to Rebecca and asked if she wanted to help to bath Isabelle. "Though we usually call her Bella."

"Oh, yes please," smiled Rebecca, "I would love to."

So John and I continued our walk whilst the two nursemaids went off with Val and another John and their children.

It was our girls' bedtime when we met again. They had both enjoyed themselves helping with the children. They had told Val that we were Chalet School fans, and were going to explore the area the books described. She was thrilled and confessed that she was a great fan and had all the Chalet School books.

Next morning we found that they had asked if they could have a table near us. The kind staff put two tables together in the bay window and we all sat together. Rebecca sat next to baby Bella and Elizabeth next to Nathanael. Everyone was happy.
The family were called Taylor-Bradford and I wondered if they were any relation to the authoress Barbara Taylor-Bradford.

"Unfortunately no," Val laughed, "although I have often been asked, and I love her books, especially the 'Woman of Substance' series."

We then found out we had more than that in common. They were Methodists and came from Derbyshire. John was thinking of training to become a local preacher and was thrilled to be able to discuss the possibilities with my John, when I explained who we were.

"Oh dear," I thought, "can't we ever get away from it?" Then another thought came. "Why should we want to get away from it?"

We had a great deal to be thankful for. We had been extremely lucky, and should be glad to share it.

The two Johns decided to go for a walk and have a good chat, whilst Val and I discussed our trip to Achensee. The girls took the children to the playroom.

"You need not worry about your little ones Val," I said. "The girls love children and are very good with them. They will be well looked after."

"I wasn't worrying" she smiled. "I knew straight away I could trust them."

Then she surprised me by asking. "What's it like being a minister's wife?"

"I can only tell you what it is like being married to John," I replied. "But why do you ask?"

Then she surprised me by saying.

"I have felt for some time that my John is being called to the Ministry."

"If God wants him to be a minister He will let him know," I assured her. "What does he do now?"

"He teaches R.E. in a big Comprehensive School. He has always loved it, but lately he has been very restless. He takes Assemblies as part of his job and wonders about being a Local Preacher, but I think he feels called to the Ministry. The only thing is, I don't think he knows that yet."

"Well, don't worry about it. If God wants him He will certainly let him know."

"That is all very well," she said. "But how on earth would we afford it?"

"O just wait and see what happens," I advised. "We had three quite young children when John felt his call, and I knew before he did. God sorted me out first and sent me to train for teaching. John became a local preacher and qualified at the same time as I did. It was at his recognition service that he knew what he had to do."

"But, if you had just qualified, how did you manage your probationary year?"

"It was more complicated than that," I told her. "However John candidated and by the time he was accepted and ready to go to college someone came and asked to buy our house. Then, when we knew he was going to Wesley College in Bristol I applied for a job. It was a good job I didn't get it, because it would have been miles from where we lived. By the way, we lived for two years in Charles Wesleys' House. I got a job quite near, and our two sons found jobs. Peter John in a bank and Nick got a job training to be an organ tuner. Then he went on to qualify as a music teacher. Charlotte Anne won a scholarship to Hunmanby Hall, a Methodist Boarding School. Then, just to show God has a sense of humour he presented us with these two. Don't you worry, if God really wants him, He will sort it all out. So try not to worry. Bye the way, do you want me to tell John what you feel?"

She thought about it for a moment and then said,

"Yes please, but when you are on your own. I won't tell my John until we get home."

When the men came back the four of us decided we would go to Achensee together, so we planned it in more detail.

CHAPTER ELEVEN

We had a wonderful time in Pertisau. It was a great thrill to go up on the cog railway, which climbed up the mountainside to Achensee (Tiernsee, in the Chalet Books.) We all swam in the lake and then enjoyed a trip on the boat which stopped at lots of little villages, where we found wonderful coffee and cakes. Having the little ones to look after certainly made the holiday even more enjoyable for our girls, and John and I found we could wander around on our own, which was a great treat for us.

I told John what Val had told me and he said
"Yes, I know."
"Oh he told you then?" I replied.
"No, he didn't. I don't think he knows yet, but he soon will." I looked up at John and laughed.
"That is quite like us isn't it? After all I knew before you did." John smiled down at me.
"God knows what He is about; sort the women out first."
"I've told John to keep in touch, and advised him to talk to his minister back home about becoming a Local Preacher."

We had booked to go on the trip to Salzburg. We both felt the girls should see as much of the city where Mozart was born as possible. Our friends hadn't booked for this as they felt the journey would be too long for little ones.

We thoroughly enjoyed every minute of the day, but it was tiring and both Elizabeth and Rebecca slept most of the way home.

We rang our older children that evening and had surprises from both Nick and Charlotte Anne. Nick said that he and Caroline planned to get engaged at Christmas and they would spend Christmas Eve with her parents, and then come on to us for the rest of Christmas.

It was Richard who answered the phone when we rang our daughter.

"Oh," he said. "Have we got news for you?" Then he called Charlotte Anne and said.

"I'll let her tell you our news."

"Guess what," she said, "our doctor says there are at least two babies. He can definitely hear at least two heartbeats. There may be more."

"What wonderful news." I beamed at the family all gathered round. "I'll let you tell them yourself."

I handed the phone to John and he held it down so the girls could hear. They screamed out

"Twins, or more, whoopee."

Rebecca's first comment was. "Well you did buy four rattles, perhaps you will need them all."

"We had better go back to the shop and buy some more" was Elizabeth's comment.

John was still talking to Charlotte Anne and she could hear all the background noise.

"Just tell my little sisters that we will want them both to be godmothers to our babies and there should be one each for them. Tell them they can choose their godchild's second name. We will trust them not to choose anything outrageous."

What a great big thrill.

"We can't exactly choose until we know whether it will be boys or girls or some of each," said Elizabeth.

"No, but we can have some ideas" answered Rebecca."

We put the telephone down after wishing them well and quite looked forward to going home.

The rest of the holiday sped by and we began to pack. We had to buy a new case to put all the presents and extra clothes we had bought in. I had bought two more rattles, as a precaution.

John telephoned Mike and told him we were expected to land about 2 o'clock. Realising that we would be some time getting through customs Mike said he would definitely be there for 2.30pm.

We looked forward to the flight home, and it was very enjoyable. We all felt we would sometime like to go on a long flight, if that were possible. We said good-bye to our new friends at the airport. We had already exchanged addresses so we could keep in touch. Then Val gave each of the girls a small parcel.

"Just to say thank you for looking after our two, they have loved it."

"But, we have enjoyed looking after them," our two chorused. When they opened the parcels later they found they each had a necklace of 'Austrian Crystal' to remind them of their holiday. They were very pleased and hoped we would all meet again.

Our flight was a little delayed but we landed at 2.30.pm and found Mike waiting for us.

He hoped we had enjoyed our holiday. Then he turned to John.

"There has certainly been some excitement whilst you were away. We are very glad to have you back."

"You had better tell me," John said. "Excitement can be either good, or bad. Which is it?"

"That all depends on your point of view," he smiled. "The builders want to start work, and that means we have to start demolishing the building pretty soon. It caused a bit of a panic, for no-one knows how we will manage without our building for perhaps a few months."

"Well, the Circuit Stewards and I have sorted all that out. You surely don't think we would leave a thing like this to chance do you?"

"No I suppose not, but we didn't know it would be so soon," he said.

"Well, don't you worry about it. I'll get things sorted as soon as I get back."

"But where on earth will we worship whilst all the demolition and re-building work is going on?"

"At 'Stepping Stones,' the special school." John informed him. "That was all sorted out long ago. The Headmaster talked to me about it as soon as I told him about our building scheme. He talked to the governors and told them he would like to offer the school hall for our worship and some classrooms for our Sunday School. They agreed and of course our Circuit Stewards were very grateful.

"People will be jolly relieved to know that," Mike smiled. "When are you telling them?"

"Goodness, let me get home and to my desk and I'll put it all in hand as a priority," John told him. "We'll call a meeting and let the members know as soon as I have told the Church Council. Will that do?"

"Certainly," smiled Mike. "I told everyone not to panic. You were sure to have arranged something."

The girls had been listening to this and thought immediately of Guides.

"What about the Uniformed Organisations and Youth Club? Then there is the Women's Meeting and things like choir practice. Gosh there will be a lot to fit in. Can everything go on as usual?"

"As much as possible" John said. "Your Mum has agreed that the Women's Meeting can fit into our lounge. There are only about fifteen of them and they can use our kitchen for their cups of tea. "

As far as Youth Club and the Uniformed Organisations are concerned they are going to use your old Primary School. The governors agreed when the Headmaster suggested that they could use the Hall.

"This has all come a little earlier than we expected, but everything is as organised as possible."

"We might have known," Mike chuckled. "I suppose really that it will be good to get started on the scheme. We have been talking about it for long enough."

We arrived home safely, and after a cup of tea, Mike left us to settle down to our unpacking. John, of course went into his study to tackle the post and other correspondence. The girls rang Pam to tell her we were back and to enquire about their pets.

"They have been as good as gold," Pam informed them, "but they will be glad to see you back. I'll pop them round after tea."

"Don't worry," they informed her, "we will come and get them." They found the box of 'Mozart' chocolates they had bought themselves for Pam and Derek and, calling out to us that they were off to get the dogs, disappeared out of the back door.

They came back with two very excited dogs. Who jumped and barked a welcome, until I shooed them into the garden.

"Auntie Pam has had news of Millie" Elizabeth told me. "She is out of hospital and seems to accept the tubes up her nose. She is feeding well and putting on weight, so they are all relieved."

"Oh that is wonderful news," I assured the girls. "I'm sure there will be lots of problems to overcome, but Millie is a very much loved little girl and will get all the help possible to help her thrive."

"Now, what are we going to do about tea? We had sandwiches for lunch so we need something a bit more substantial."

John came into the kitchen and heard my question.

"No, we don't have to worry," he smiled. "Margery Branston has phoned to say she has a meal all ready for us, and will 6 o'clock be all right?"

"Oh wonderful, but just like her," I smiled. "Get washed and changed everyone and please somebody find the rattles. One of them is for William, their new grandson. He will just be old enough to hold it now."

"I'm only part way through the pile of post," John said, "but Norman will put me in the picture about the demolition. Quite a lot is junk mail. But there is one great piece of news. The Rank Trust have granted our request and will fund it as soon as demolition starts. That will be an enormous help. Norman will be delighted and he will soon work out how much we still have to raise."

Margery had a lovely roast dinner with all the trimmings waiting for us and I must say we did it justice. Norman took John off to his study and we women cleared away and washed up.

"I'll wash," I offered, "the twins will dry and you can put away whilst we talk." We talked non-stop.

The men joined us for coffee and the girls fussed Jess, their beautiful Golden Retriever. Norman was delighted about the grant and asked John about 'The Stewardship' project.

This was all ready to be put into operation in September and involved not only members, but also anyone interested in taking part. The project suggested that people were asked to give, not only money, but also their time, and their talents. Everyone was given a form to fill in stating regular giving, time they were prepared to give to the church, such as cleaning and maintenance, help with the organisations, preparing drinks and biscuits after worship, running events such as quiz evenings, musical events, or social occasions. One family said they would run a 'pudding evening.' They would sell tickets and offer three different puddings and a drink for the price.

Another bright idea came from our friend Margery. Whilst we were talking at her house after our holiday, she suggested a circuit cookery book. We would ask people for favourite family recipes. Then get someone to design a cover. We could call it 'The Cotteswold Cookery Book'. We all thought it was a lovely idea.

Elizabeth said, "We could ask people to make up their recipe and have a sale of the goodies along with the book."

"That should go down well, as well as making a good launch of the book. Well done." I said.

After a meeting with The Circuit Stewards and representatives from The Property Division, the final amount the Circuit would have to find was twenty three thousand pounds.

John called a meeting of his Church Stewards, and they arranged a Church Meeting for the first week in September. This would probably be the last one to be held in the present building.

CHAPTER TWELVE

We arrived home just in time to welcome our new granddaughter. Alexandra Katy Williams made her appearance on 22nd July, two days before our Wedding Anniversary. She was quite a contrast to her big sister. Emma was fair gold like our girls. Alexandra was dark and I thought she was like Mum, although no one else could see the likeness. She was bigger than Emma and very noisy. Vanessa said she had kept the whole nursery awake during the night. We all had a cuddle and Emma was not put out by the fussing, for she had her share from all of us. Peter John was taking two weeks leave to look after her, and we told Vanessa we would be glad to help in any way.

The twins had, of course, had their birthday present with the visit to Pertisau whilst we were on holiday, but they still had a party to look forward to. They decided they would have it on the tenth of August so we could go and see Charlotte Anne and Richard on their actual birthday, the twelfth.

They asked if they could have a swimming party, with a picnic in the park afterwards. They each invited six friends. A great time was had by all. They all enjoyed swimming and there was a terrific noise. Luckily it was a beautiful day and the picnic was very successful.

They had chosen pasties with lots of crisps and savoury bits, followed by birthday cake, and ice cream from the ice cream van in the park. Drink was easy, a choice of bottles of fruit drinks, and lemonade, from plastic cups. Everything could then be thrown in the bin.

Dad had arrived with my brother and his wife and children the day before. He was being very brave, but I knew he was missing Mum so much. Somehow he had lost his sparkle.

He didn't fancy the swimming part of the party, so John fetched him once we arrived at the park, and he said he enjoyed the picnic. John took him for a stroll around the park whilst the girls and their friends enjoyed the swings and slide for a while.

When the last of the parents had collected their girls, we piled the rugs and the dogs into the back and drove home.

"Now," Dad said, "you haven't had my present yet. I didn't have a clue about shopping for you, but I thought you might like to have a meal out. We are going to 'The Tara' if that is all right for you."

"Wow," they said together. "That's posh."

"Well then go and have a wash and change and we will go out to dinner at 7 o'clock."

We were all delighted. John, of course knew all about it, as Dad had asked him to book somewhere rather special for the five of us when he could be free. John had kept the tenth free for the girls, as well as the twelfth for our visit to Charlotte Anne and Richard.

It was a lovely end to the day and we all enjoyed a delicious meal in the restaurant. The girls chose to go modern and had Indian food. Dad chose roast beef and Yorkshire pudding, whilst John and I had steak and chips. After the dessert course we went into the lounge and had coffee and nibbles. The girls, of course, chose diet coke.

We sat for a long time, looking out over the river and saw a kingfisher flash by. Dad told us that he would like to stay with us until the end of August and then go back to 'Westerley' for the winter. He knew that if ever he wanted us he only had to ring.

"But, you are all so busy" he said. John then told him that whatever was happening we were available for him.

"You must promise us that you will ring us. You are our first priority," he told him.

Dad promised and then wanted to know arrangements for going to Birmingham on the twelfth.

We explained that we had arranged with Pam that she would collect Toffee and Fudge the night before. We also told him that we were hoping to be off as soon as possible after we got up.

"We like to stop for breakfast on the motorway," I told him. "It saves time and gives John a break."

Dad said he thought that was a good idea and he would be up bright and early. "Don't worry your heads about me," he assured us.

We put our alarm on, as insurance, but we were awake at 6.30am and John went to run our bath whilst I made a cup of tea for everyone. The girls and Dad were all awake when I took the morning tea up, and we were all dressed and ready to go by 7.15am; before the post arrived with the rest of the twins birthday cards.

The roads were not busy at that time and we were at the service station before 8 o'clock. We enjoyed our cooked breakfast and a drink, and we were refreshed and ready to set off on the last lap of the journey.

We arrived at the flat just after 9.30 am and John parked round the back in the car park whilst we went up in the lift. Imagine John's surprise when we all arrived back in the car park. There was a note left for us in Richard's handwriting saying.

'Go straight to Maternity ward. Babies on the way.'

We all piled back into the car a bit excited and yet subdued. It was about six weeks early and a bit of a worry.

I explained to everyone that we might not be allowed to see Charlotte Anne. It depended on her condition. They all understood. The rest of the journey, which wasn't far, was a bit quiet. We were all busy with our own thoughts.

When we arrived I went to the desk to enquire and was told to wait whilst they found out what was happening.

Richard came into the waiting room looking harassed. He told us that Charlotte Anne had woken in the early hours with labour pains. He had rung the hospital and explained what was happening and was told to bring her in straight away.

"We got here pretty sharpish I can tell you, and they put Charlotte Anne into a room in the private ward. That's my perk he grinned." A consultant examined her and confirmed that she was in the first stages of labour. Because they are expecting a multiple birth they set up a team to look after her and the babies."

"Try not to worry," he said. "Everything is going according to plan. Charlotte Anne is on gas and air and she wants to see you, but don't stay long."

"I think we should go one at a time," I said, and Richard agreed.

We went up in the lift to the ward and everyone stayed outside whilst Richard went in to see what was happening. The bed was empty and a nurse came hurrying along to say Charlotte Anne was in the delivery room and asking for Richard.

We stayed where we were, and a nurse kindly came to explain that the babies were determined to be born quickly. She asked if we would like a cup of coffee and suggested we go into the waiting room. A maid brought a tray with a pot of coffee, cups and milk and sugar along with a plate of biscuits. I needed the coffee, but couldn't eat anything. Elizabeth told the nurse who came to see if we were all right, that she intended to be a nurse.

The nurse smiled at her and said "I'll see if I can find someone to show you round if you like." Elizabeth jumped up eagerly.

"Oh, yes please. Any chance of seeing my sister?"

"Sorry that is not possible at the moment, although the rate she is going, you may be able to before long." Then she looked at me.

"Are you her Mum?"

"Yes" I answered.

"Well she is asking for you. How do you feel?"

"Great," I said, jumping up.

Leaving the rest, I followed the nurse along the corridor and into the delivery room and heard my daughter groaning. It was all so familiar, I could feel my stomach clench as I remembered the pains of childbirth.

Richard was holding the gas and air machine over her nose, so I grabbed her hot hand in mine and felt her pushing hard.

The mid-wife beckoned to Richard to come and watch his first baby being born.

It was a boy, and although he looked tiny he looked strong, and gave a loud scream as he arrived into the world. They just had time to wrap him in a towel and show Charlotte Anne her son, when his brother arrived. He looked different, but healthy and certainly strong and kicking.

"Thank goodness that's over," smiled Charlotte Anne, beaming at the two babies Richard was holding close to her.

Then she groaned. "There's another pain coming" as she grabbed my hand.

Into the world slipped another baby. This time it was a daughter. She looked like a miniature Charlotte Anne. She had the same colouring and the same shaped face. She looked smaller than her brothers, but just as healthy.

"Please tell me that is the last," asked a weary Charlotte Anne. "I really couldn't do that again."

"That is the lot," she was assured. The triplets were all put into incubators.

"Just as a precaution" the Consultant assured us. "They are three healthy little babies, but they are premature, and just need a little help with their breathing."

Charlotte Anne kissed them and then surprised us all.

"Please let me see the rest of my family."

The nurse tidied her up and said

"By all means, if you feel up to it."

She was wheeled into her own room and John, the twins, and Dad joined us.

Of course everyone was thrilled, and terribly excited, and longing to see Charlotte Anne as well as the new babies.

A nurse came in and brought a cup of tea for Charlotte Anne and Richard. The rest of us assured her we had just had coffee. Then we were taken into the Intensive Care Baby Unit where we found our three little ones. They all had tubes and this worried the twins, but the nurse re-assured them that they wouldn't need help for long.

Each incubator had a label stating 'Baby Denson 1, 2 and 3.'

"Have you got names yet?" asked the nurse. Charlotte Anne told her that we were going back to her room to decide on names. She told us that son number one was going to be called after her Dad.

"But we thought we would have a change and call him not just John but Jonathan. He will also be Mark after Richard's brother, his godfather. Our other little son is going to be Daniel William after both his great grandfathers. Now girls, what about your goddaughter? What have you chosen for her."

"I would like her to have my second name, Claire" said Rebeccca.

"Very appropriate, since I chose that name for you" smiled Charlotte Anne. And what about you Elizabeth?

"I think Claire Louise sounds nice," she said. "I don't think Claire Helen would sound right." We all agreed.

"So. Jonathan Mark, Daniel William, and Claire Louise. Does everyone agree?" We all did, and so did Tom and Marion who had just arrived.

"All the names go very well with Denson" Marion said "and my Dad is going to be thrilled to have Daniel called after him, and so will Mark."

Everyone was happy and so the baby's names were stuck onto their incubators. I could tell that Charlotte Anne was very tired and suggested that we leave her with Richard, and go and see about lunch.

"The hospital has an excellent restaurant." Richard told us. "Go to the lifts and it's on the top floor. When you come back a probationer nurse is willing to show Elizabeth round and tell her about training."

We all had an excellent lunch and talked non-stop about babies, for we told Tom and Marion about Alexandra's arrival.

"She looks enormous compared to these three little mites." I explained. "I can't wait to get them all together for a photograph."

We asked where the public telephones were so that we could let everyone know about the new arrivals. Then we had a lovely surprise. The probationary nurse arrived and it was our own niece, Carey Jane.

"I've just been to see Charlotte Anne," she smiled "and guess what? I got a peep at the babies. Aren't they sweet? I just wanted to scoop them up and give them a big cuddle. Of course I wasn't allowed. But do you know what, little Claire Louise had to be untangled. She had wrapped her little legs around the tubing and was trying to climb up them."

"All the nurses laughed, and said. We will have to watch this little gymnast."

Then she asked us about Alexandra Katy and told us we would have to have a family party when the triplets were allowed out.

"What a celebration," she said "and on your twelfth birthday and their parents' wedding anniversary. They have certainly caused a stir. What a lot to celebrate on the glorious twelfth."

CHAPTER THIRTEEN

It was hard to settle down to normality after all the excitement of our new grandchildren, but then what was ever normal in our house? Granny D and Irene wanted us to have tea with them and hear all about the new babies. John had plenty to think about concerning the demolition and re-building of the church, and the twins and I had to think about the new school year. They would go back as second year pupils and I must think about my new Transition.

I had decided to use John's study in the afternoons when he was out visiting, or at meetings. After lunch was cleared away, I thought I would get some peace to do some preparation before thinking about the evening meal. Well, that is what I planned.

The first afternoon I had just sat down with my new timetable when the telephone rang. I should have switched on the answering machine.

My caller wanted to arrange a wedding. I explained that my husband would ring her when he came in, but that wouldn't do.

" I have to book the reception and flowers as well as taxis and I need to know now," she said. "I really need to book the first Saturday in October. Can't you just put it in his diary?"

"No I certainly cannot," I explained. "You will have to speak to my husband first and he will not be in until about 5.30 pm. I will tell him you called."

I knew for certain that John would not agree to hold a wedding on that Saturday. The next day would be Harvest Festival and the church would be full of people decorating the church. Then I had a fit of giggles. That is if there is a church here to decorate. Would it have been demolished by then?

The girls were out swimming with some school friends, and then they were invited back to tea with them. I was picking them up about 7 o'clock and John and I were having tea with Dad. Anyway that was the plan.

I was sorting out a mathematics syllabus for my new Transition Form when the doorbell rang. I answered the door to a very unhappy pair. A lady somewhere in her mid-forties I guessed, stood with a teenage girl. They were both crying and looking thoroughly confused.

"Come in" I said and ushered them into the lounge.

"I just don't know what to do," the lady said, "but I thought you might help us."

"I certainly will, if I can," I assured her offering them the settee.

"You won't know us," the lady said, "but I know you and your husband are well thought of, and I just didn't know where to go."

"Tell me your names and what the problem is, then I may be able to help. I certainly will if I can."

"My name is Phoebe Matthews and this is my daughter Jennifer, always called Jenny. I couldn't get her up this morning, and when I turned her over in bed her face was tear stained. Of course I wanted to know what was the matter. She told me what had happened, and I just could not believe what she was saying. She told me she thought she might be pregnant."

"Oh you poor loves," I said. "Let me get you both a hot drink. What would you like, coffee, tea, chocolate?"

"Chocolate please," sniffed Jenny, "but Mum would rather have coffee."

I left them and went into the kitchen to put on the kettle and a pan of milk. Then I was baffled. What on earth does one do about this? I needed John.

I took the drinks in with a plate of biscuits and found them hugging each other, but still crying. They took their drinks with shaking hands, but refused the biscuits.

"Are you sure?" I asked. "Have you seen a doctor for instance?"

"We haven't seen anyone yet. I really am completely stunned."

Jenny began crying again and I tried to comfort her.

"What makes you think you might be pregnant?" I asked. "Your period might just be late you know."

Jenny just sobbed again and I asked her Mum how old she was.

"Just sixteen," she said, and then wrapping her sobbing daughter in her arms she sobbed with her.

"Look," I said, "this is a shock for you both, but you are not alone. We will help you through this, and you will find others will be there for you. The important thing is to see your doctor first and get it confirmed. Then you will be in the system and be told what to do."

I was told who their doctor was, and asked if I could possibly tell her what was suspected. I said I was quite happy to ring Dr. Morrison, a very kind lady doctor who I knew would help Jenny.

I went out into the hall to make the call when John came in looking very odd, and covering his left eye.

"What's wrong?" I asked, feeling very worried.

"I have no idea. It doesn't hurt, but something is certainly wrong. I cannot see properly out of that eye. Everything is hazy."

I sat him down in the kitchen and explained about the two people in the lounge.

"Just let me make this call, and then I had better ring our doctor for an emergency appointment."

Jenny's doctor was very understanding and told me to send them straight round to her, and she would see them as soon as possible.

They were very grateful and said they would let me know what happened.

Then I rang our doctor.

He said. "It sounds to me as though John has a detached retina. It's no good wasting time coming here. It would be better to go straight to casualty and get someone to examine him as soon as possible."

I called in on Dad and explained.

"I'm coming with you" he insisted.

I thought I had better pack pyjamas, sponge bag and shaving equipment in case they kept John in, as I thought they might. I rang the mother of our daughters' friend and explained that we had been called out on an emergency, but didn't say what it was.

"That's fine," she said. "The girls are having a good time here and I'll keep them until you get back."

We set off for the Casualty Department. John sat beside me looking very worried, and Dad sat in the back. It didn't take long, and I dropped John and Dad at the hospital door whilst I parked the car in the multi-storey car park.

I told John to walk steadily to the eye department and explain what had happened.

"I'll find you," I assured them.

John did not have to wait. As soon as he explained the problem he was taken to see a specialist, and was with him when I arrived.

"You will have to be admitted" the specialist told him. "You have a detached retina, and must have it seen to as soon as possible."

"But I can't" John began. He was cut short.

"No buts" the specialist said. "I'll operate as soon as possible."

Dad and I looked at each other. How on earth were we going to persuade John that he was staying here, and for the next week or so?

Then the specialist took it out of our hands.

"Let me explain what has happened to your eye."

John could not argue with that. He either had an operation, or he would lose the sight of his eye.

Dad said. "Give me your diary John and I'll contact your colleagues. I can take your Sunday services if necessary. No one is indispensable. I know it's difficult, but somehow or other we will manage."

John was admitted and told he would be operated on as soon as possible. We saw him settled in bed and told him we would stay until we knew what was happening.

When John was taken to theatre Dad and I went home. I rang Elizabeth and Rebecca, and told them what had happened, and that I would pick them up as soon as possible. Their friend's Mum Jill, took the phone from them and said,

"Don't come, I'll bring them home. Just let me know when you are ready." I was very grateful.

I rang our older children, but told Richard not to tell Charlotte Anne until he thought it was all right. She had enough to worry about with her babies, although they were all putting on weight and not causing any problems except Claire, who was constantly tying herself in her tubing, and causing much hilarity amongst the nursing staff.

Peter John and Nick both said, "We'll come", but I explained that it was better to wait and see what their Dad was like when he came round. I promised to keep them informed.

Then I rang Norman, our Senior Circuit Steward. He was shocked, but told me not to worry ringing anyone else. He would see to it all. I told him Dad would take Sunday's services and he was grateful for that.

Dad gave me a big hug. "Try not to worry" he said. "The surgeon is one of the best, I'm told. Let's go and have something to eat and by that time John may be back in the ward."

I felt I couldn't eat a thing, but Dad said. "You have to stay strong darling, both for the children and the church. John is in good hands and will need you when he comes round from the anaesthetic."

We went back to the hospital restaurant and I managed a coffee and two slices of toast. Dad had a sandwich and a cup of tea. Then we went to John's ward. They were just bringing him back and I was thankful to see that apart from a plaster over his left eye, he looked quite well.

The sister, who knew John well, said she would take great care of him. They would keep him very still for the next few hours, but we could ring later for more information. She could not say yet how long John would be kept in, but told me he would be off work for about a month.

We went home and as news filtered through we were inundated with telephone calls and messages.

Dad said. "Put that machine of yours on. Then send for the girls. What we all need is a good night's sleep. Don't forget we have all had a shock."

I rang to say we were at home and ready for the girls. There was a lot of explaining to do, for both girls kept asking questions.

"What on earth is a detached retina?" they wanted to know. I explained as well as I could.

"But what caused it?" asked Rebecca.

"Has Dad bumped his head or something like that?" asked Elizabeth.

I had no idea, for I had not had time to question him, but I didn't think so.

"Apparently, it can just happen, perhaps through stress."

"Well, there is plenty of that just now," Dad said, "but when isn't there?"

We all had an evening drink and decided an early bed was best for all of us.

"I'll just get the latest report from the hospital" I told everyone. "Then we are all going to bed."

The report was the best news we could have. John had come round and was comfortable.

"He just needs to be kept quiet and very still" I was told. "Because we must all be very careful, he is in a private room and will stay there until he is discharged."

We felt he was in good hands and went to bed. What a day this had been.

CHAPTER FOURTEEN

Messages of good will, cards and flowers arrived, as well as people arriving to see how they could help. Pam and Derek arrived and asked if I would like them to take the dogs.

"We will have the twins as well if that would help" Pam offered. We said thanks, but no to both offers. The girls are happier here and the dogs are no trouble. They were, in fact a comfort to us all. Then Pam said

"Write out a shopping list as well as jobs to be done and we will see to it." This was a wonderful offer, which I accepted gratefully.

"The biggest job is answering the telephone" I said. "People naturally want to know what is happening, and I can't just leave the answering machine on."

"Let me plonk myself by the phone" Derek said. "As long as I get fed and watered every so often I'll be fine, and I can tell people the latest news about John."

"I'll do the housework and make the meals," Pam offered.

What great friends they are, and such a comfort to have around.

We were able to visit John at any time, as long as we understood that he must be kept quiet and still. Most importantly, he must not be worried about anything.

We took all the cards in, but the nurse said.

"Where on earth am I going to put them? Look at this lot."

Strings had been put all around his bed. It looked like Christmas.

John was able to talk to us and we passed on the messages of good will and offers of help. We told him we were not allowed to speak about work, but assured him that everything was going smoothly and all he had to worry about was getting better.

"For goodness sake, John, accept rest and quiet. You won't often get that, you know," Dad told him.

I told him the latest news of all our grandchildren, and laughed when I explained how little Claire kept getting tangled up in her tubes.

"She is going to be quite a little character, I can see it coming," John smiled.

The girls told John about their day with their friends, and how they were looking forward to going back to school.

"Gosh, we'll be in second year." Then they explained where their new form room would be and that their new form mistress was Mrs. Tucker. Mrs. Day would teach them for R.E. and history this year, so they were pleased about that.

We told John we would visit twice a day, afternoon and evening. "But we cannot stay long, for you are not to get excited or tired by visitors." I told him that Derek was in charge of the telephone and was doing a great job, keeping people informed.

"He is also taking messages, but those can wait until you are back in business."

We had taken John a personal tape recorder, and tapes of books he would enjoy. He could see well enough with one eye, and I wondered if there was anything else he would like brought in.

"Well," he said, "I could be preparing sermons." I disabused him of that idea.

"You are not to even think about work," I told him, "so forget it, and pretend you are on holiday."

I gave him news of all our family, and told him they would come and see him as soon as possible, but one family at a time. All he asked for were some oranges.

"I get so thirsty" he said. "A nice juicy orange would go down a treat."

We left him after putting clean pyjamas and a box of tissues in his locker. I knew Norman and Margery were coming in to see him. They assured me that work would not be mentioned except to tell him that there was nothing to worry about. It was all in hand.

When we got home Derek had a few messages to pass on. One was from the lady who had rung about a date for her wedding. Derek had sensibly told her that John was not available and given her the name and number of one of the other ministers in the Circuit. Another message was from Phoebe, thanking us for our help and saying she would ring me later to explain what had happened. All other messages were about John, and Derek was able to answer those.

Norman and Margery were coming to see us after they had visited John. I looked at the desk and saw my mathematics syllabus staring at me. I turned it over. It would just have to wait.

I was talking to Nick when Norman and Margery arrived. Nick told me he and Caroline were coming the next day and would come home first and get directions before visiting John.

Norman had great news. John was behaving himself and getting well quickly. He had not been allowed up yet, but was propped up on pillows and allowed to reach for things like his tape recorder and the newspaper.

Then he said. "I didn't tell John, of course, but I have heard from the demolition people and they want to start at the end of the month. There will be no Harvest in church this year, but John had arranged it all with our special school, and they are quite thrilled to have the Harvest Festival there. They are even thinking of making it a joint event and taking part. Alan has agreed to take the service, so it should be a great occasion."

I had a word with John's surgeon when I next visited. He was just leaving and I rushed after him.

"Look," I said, "I understand that we must not discuss work, but I know John, and he will not be able to just forget about it. If I give him snippets of good news would that be all right?"

He thought about it for a moment. "Such as?" he asked.

Then I told him about the demolition squad moving in and how services were going to be arranged.

"That's fine," he said. "Good news won't hurt him. I'll leave it to you. As long as he doesn't get excited."

"Better not let Nick near him," I thought. Then I knew better. Nick knew his Dad must not get excited and he would be very careful. 'Arsenal' and its problems would interest, but not excite John.

A bigger problem was the flowers. People were very kind and arrived with flowers, but what to do with them was getting to be a problem. All my vases were full and the house looked like a flower shop. All the Circuit churches sent their contributions, but not only that, the Anglican and Catholic churches sent displays with good wishes and assurances of their prayers. Pam solved the problem.

"Why not keep them for a day or two and then send them to the hospice and old people's homes?"

What a good idea. Each day, as more arrived Derek and Pam piled previous offerings in their car and deposited them to various places. Some went to lonely people we knew of, and this way many people benefited, whilst we still had plenty to cheer us.

The next post brought a picture of our three new babies. They had been put together on a mattress, Claire in the middle of her two brothers. Jonathan was looking very serious as though he were trying to solve lots of problems. Daniel was just contented. Claire had both feet in the air and looked as though she was trying to wave at us. It was a beautiful picture and I knew John would be very proud of it. We also had a picture of Emma with Alexandra on her knee. I would take both photographs into the hospital, and John could have them on his locker. How proudly he would show off his beautiful grandchildren. That would do him the world of good.

CHAPTER FIFTEEN

John was in hospital for ten days. He had gradually been allowed to do more each day. On the last day he had been allowed to go for a shower and then get dressed. He said it felt wonderful. After breakfast he was told he could go home, providing he promised to be sensible. He would not be able to drive for a few weeks, and he certainly must not lift anything heavy.

"Go steady, and begin to work a little at a time," the surgeon said. "I'll see you in a fortnight and see how you are then."

John rang me immediately and said "Come and get me, as soon as possible."

I assured him I was on my way, and called out to everyone the good news. Derek assured us that they would stay for the rest of the day.

"Just go and get him home," he smiled, "and we'll have the kettle on."

I called out to the girls and Dad, and they all appeared in the hall.

"Can we come?" the girls asked, but Dad sensibly said

"It's better if we clear up here and put the fire on. Then we can welcome him home in private." So that is what happened.

I was at the hospital half-an-hour after getting the message. John was ready with his case packed. His bandages were off and apart from looking a bit shaky he was his old self. A nurse carried his case, and came with us to the door. I left John sitting down and went to get the car. We were soon on our way and it was wonderful to have John beside me. I had missed him so much.

We were welcomed home with a cheerful fire and coffee and biscuits ready for us.

"Oh, it's so good to be back" John smiled at us all as he enjoyed his coffee and biscuits. He thanked Pam and Derek and said,

"Just give me a little time to adjust and then I will want to know all that is happening."

We told him then about the demolition at the end of the month and that his services were covered until the end of September. However, we relented a little and told him he would be allowed to take part in the last service in the present building. Pastoral work must wait a little longer. His colleagues were covering that, and he was assured that there was nothing too pressing anyway.

Norman had taken over the overseeing of the demolition, and was dealing with the firm doing the building and the refurbishment in the Docks. There was absolutely nothing to worry about as far as the Circuit was concerned.

He could see for himself that his grandchildren were doing well, and everyone else in the family was fine. He had spoken on the telephone to his parents and his sister, and they were all delighted to know he was doing well and back home. Peter John, Vanessa, and the two little girls were coming on Saturday, Nick and Caroline were coming on Sunday. We promised John that if all went well, we would take him to see Charlotte Anne, Richard, and the triplets the following weekend. He was quite content.

After coffee I could see that he looked a little drowsy and suggested he went for a rest on the bed whilst I saw to lunch. Pam had put a chicken casserole in the oven and I thought baked potatoes would be a good idea, followed by a crumble.

He agreed and went up to the bedroom, followed by Dad and our daughters.

After dealing with a few domestic jobs I telephoned a few people to let them know John was home. A few visitors would be good for him, but not all at once, so I arranged a few visits with plenty of time for rests in between.

A few days later I suggested a trip out, with perhaps coffee and cakes at our favourite teashop in Burford. We all enjoyed doing normal things again, especially John, who said he was feeling much stronger. He was certainly eating and sleeping well.

John said that getting up and having breakfast were quite enough for a morning, but after lunch and a snooze he felt he could begin working for a while. Perhaps prepare some sermons.

I agreed, so the pattern for the day for the time being, was a rest after breakfast, perhaps a visitor or two for coffee, lunch, then a rest. After lunch a trip in the car to the park, or a beauty spot, afternoon tea, sometimes with friends, followed by a quiet evening reading or watching television, and a fairly early bed.

One afternoon we went to visit Irene and Granny D. They were thrilled to see the photographs of all our grandchildren. Granny D laughed at Claire's antics. Then she spotted what I had seen immediately. How like John little Jonathan was.

"He looks just like you do when you are preaching," she said. "I wonder?"

"Now don't go putting a clerical collar on the poor child" smiled John. "But, you can tell he is a thinker. He and Daniel are not a bit alike are they?"

"No they are not, but Jonathan and Claire have the same golden hair. Now where does that come from I wonder? Here is another strange thing. Emma and Claire look more alike than Emma and Alexandra."

"That's true, John agreed, and it all comes from my ancestry. The Vikings, so I am led to believe."

"Are you going to have a wholesale christening of all four new babies?" Granny wanted to know.

"We haven't talked about it yet," John told her. "We have to wait until the triplets are a little older. Anyway Peter John and Vanessa may want their own service. Wherever that may be, of course."

Another day we had tea with Pam and Derek and were given a progress report on little Millie. We were delighted to know she was doing well and putting on weight. Pam showed us the latest photograph and apart from tubes in her nose she looked like any other bright and happy baby of her age. She was sitting up and certainly taking notice. What a relief.

Norman and Margery invited us for lunch one day and Norman was able to tell John more about the demolition and the sale of the bricks. Norman asked John what he thought about keeping one as a keepsake. John thought about it and then came up with an idea.

"What about keeping about a dozen and making a pattern of them when the new building goes up?"

We all liked that idea. Elizabeth suggested making the pattern of a cross on the front of the new church and Norman said he would suggest it at the next Property Meeting.

The next Friday John had his appointment with his surgeon and was delighted with his findings. He was given permission to travel to Birmingham to see his grandchildren as long as he didn't drive. John asked him how long he thought that would be.

"Give it another two weeks and then have a short drive on a quiet road somewhere and see how you feel," he said.

John was quite content with that, and we rang Charlotte Anne to tell her. She was very excited.

"What a day this is" she said.

We asked her why? She told us that the babies were all putting on weight and no problems had been discovered when their specialist had checked them.

"We can bring them home" she said. Then she told us that everything was ready in the flat. "I have three little baskets, and three little chairs all ready for them. We have Piles of nappies, as well as all the other equipment. I think Richard and I will have to squash into the lounge. There won't be room for us."

Then she told us they were looking for a house as near to the hospital as possible. She was also thinking about giving in her notice.

"I cannot go and leave my babies," she said. "Anyhow I am managing to breast feed them all, and I will continue as long as possible."

Jonathan, the smallest was now 4lbs 2oz. Daniel was 4lbs.8oz. Claire was almost 5lbs. Hopefully, they would all be home next time we saw them. We could all have a cuddle. We couldn't wait.

CHAPTER SIXTEEN

We had an enjoyable weekend, first with Peter John, Vanessa and our little granddaughters Emma and Alexandra. Emma finds it hard to say Alexandra, and calls her Lexi. I think it will stick. Emma is very sweet with her little sister and the baby certainly knows her and kicks and gurgles at her. Mum had finished the blanket she was knitting, and it was tucked around Alexandra in her baby chair. I had found the pattern and was now on my third blanket for the triplets.

Nick and Caroline came next day and we heard all about her Aromatherapy course. It sounds fascinating. They were all anxious to hear news about their new nieces and nephews. Caroline said

"Next time we all get together we must have a large photograph."

They were all relieved to see John looking pretty normal, and warned about getting back to work too soon. I assured them that I would see he didn't and that people were being very good.

"They are enjoying him as a friend, not as their minister at the moment. There is a big difference you know."

On the following Saturday we had our trip to Birmingham. John suggested I drive the 'Bluebird'. It's bigger and more comfortable for all of us. Pam and Derek were seeing to Toffee and Fudge.

So I drove with John beside me. Dad sat with the girls in the back. We put coats and the presents we had bought to welcome the babies home in the boot. There was plenty of room. Dad insisted on buying the petrol and I had gone to the garage to fill up whilst the family did the washing up.

It is an easy drive to Birmingham, as we are only about fifteen minutes from the motorway. We stopped for coffee at the service station, and I noticed the price of petrol as we went in for coffee. I was glad I had filled up previously.

We were soon on our way again and I could feel John's agitation. Perhaps next week I would take him out somewhere quiet, and let him have a go at driving.

Charlotte Anne opened the door and we could hear the delightful sounds of babies crying. They were all in little chairs in the lounge and we couldn't wait to hold them.

The twins gave their triplet niece and nephews their presents, which their Mother took for them. Apart from the rattles there was an outfit each. A 'Winnie the Pooh' romper each, although all of a different design. They were not very impressed, but their parents loved them.

Dad gave them a cheque and told them he would like to open a bank account for each of them.

"I'll put something in each month for them, as I do for Emma and Alexandra. When they are older they should have a nice little nest egg. I don't know how long I will live, of course, but as long as I can, then I will."

Charlotte Anne and Richard gave him a hug and said a big 'Thank You.'

"You had better not think of going anywhere." Charlotte Anne said. "We all need you."

We all had a turn holding the babies and they seemed to enjoy it. I wanted all three together, so Charlotte Anne put Claire in my right arm and the two little boys in my left. Richard went to get his camera whilst Charlotte Anne explained.

"Claire is a great wriggler and you have to hold her tight. The boys are much quieter and you can manage them in one arm. Make sure you talk to Jonathan. He seems to understand every word. Daniel just enjoys a cuddle. They all three like to be sung to. Perhaps they are musical."

John was plonked in a big chair and he had his turn with all three. Then the girls had their turn.

Dad said "I'll have one at a time please." Then he told Charlotte Anne that it didn't seem that long ago, since he had held her for the first time on the day she was born on his birthday.

"And you know, she could be the same child, she is very like you."

I had told Charlotte Anne that lunch was our treat. I decided that on this occasion, a take-away would be a better idea than going out to lunch, with all that entailed.

Richard said. "We have a very good fish and chip shop just around the corner. It's quite as good as your medieval shop."

We all agreed, and sent the three men off to purchase haddock and chips for seven, whilst we put the kettle on, and plates to warm. I fetched a large plum crumble and a pot of cream from the boot whilst my daughters saw to the table.

I also brought from the boot two of the blankets Mum had knitted. I told Charlotte Anne that I would knit another one as soon as I could. Mum had finished the one for Vanessa's baby and one for Charlotte Anne. Another one just had the border to finish, which I had done. It wouldn't take me long to knit another one.

I had explained that we would not stay long after lunch, as John would need a rest when we got home. We enjoyed our lunch together and I left a coffee and walnut cake and some shortbread for Charlotte Anne and Richard to enjoy for their tea.

We rang them when we arrived home and told them how much we had enjoyed our time with them.

The dogs were brought home and Pam and Derek stayed for a cup of tea. Then Derek told John that he had worked out a pattern over the next few afternoons.

"What is that then?" asked John.

"I'll come and take you for a short drive" said Derek. "We'll see how you feel, and if everything is all right we will lengthen the drive and the difficulty until you feel ready for the motorway. How does that sound?"

"Great," answered John. "When can we start?"

"What about tomorrow afternoon after your rest, say 3 o'clock?"

John was delighted and I knew I could trust him not to go too far. The next afternoon Derek was on time and the two friends set off for a short drive. Derek hung back whilst John got the car out.

"Don't worry if we are not back as soon as you think we should be. I have arranged a small party for him. We are going to Alan's house and the rest of the staff will be there. No business talk will be allowed. But we thought he might like to meet his colleagues, and share a cup of tea with them."

I thought that was a great idea, and knew John would enjoy it.

They arrived home in time for our evening meal and John looked better for his outing. He said he had certainly enjoyed driving his car and not found any problems. He was surprised, and very pleased to be taken to tea at Alan's manse and find his other staff there. They had had a great time. He had not driven home, but was looking forward to his next trip out.

Whilst John was out with Derek I was able to use his desk. I must begin to think about next term. I would have eighteen girls in September. Five of them would be boarders. I always tried to give my boarders a little extra mothering. They were only ten and some were a very long way from home. Most of them were the daughters of men in the forces, although two of them were farmers' children.

I thought I would invite them home, perhaps twice in the term. Our girls would entertain them and they could enjoy a family meal.

The syllabus was much the same as last years, except geography, which was going to be about our coastline. We would begin at the tip of Cornwall and travel up the west coast to the tip of Scotland. Then travel back down the east coast until we reached Cornwall again. We were to look at local industries on our way round.

I would certainly have to do some studying myself, but it would be quite interesting, I hoped.

The other subjects would cause no problems I knew, and I would have time to teach my older girls. I was also teaching some second and third year R.E. along with a few girls who were studying R.E. at 'A' level. I was looking forward to it.

Dad had decided that it was time to go back to 'Westerley'. He missed his friends, and he knew he could come to us, or the boys, at any time.

Just before we went back to school, John had his longest drive down the motorway to Bridgwater. Then I took over and drove the rest of the way to Minehead. We saw Dad settled well, and returned. John said he thought he had done enough driving, so I drove back. Elizabeth said, "as soon as I am eighteen I would like to learn to drive." Rebecca assured us that she would too.

On the way back we discussed the new school year and the possibility of Rebecca having a trampoline. She had joined the 'Gloucester Springers, and knew she would love to compete. Her trainer had told her she had a good chance of winning medals at her own level. John said we would ask her advice about buying a trampoline for the garden.

School began in the middle of September and John was looking forward to starting work gradually. The last service in the church before demolition was at the end of September and this was the first time he would preach since his operation.

One of our own local preachers was leading the service and they worked together on organising it. John said he would like Benedick to take part, although he didn't say why.

This was likely to be a memorable service, and a full church was anticipated.

Demolition was to begin the next day and we wondered how long it would take, and how much mess it would make.

Elizabeth's idea of making a cross with some of the old bricks had been agreed, and John was told to choose twelve bricks from the rubble. The rest were going to a firm who were refurbishing buildings in the Docks.

School began for the girls and me on Tuesday eighteenth September, and we were all looking forward to it.

I met my new Transition in the playground. Some had come up from our own J3, although most were new girls. They looked so young and immature compared to my last Transition, but then this happens at the beginning of every school year. I led them in and welcomed them.

"You are the new Transition," I told them, "and top of the Junior School."

I explained their new timetable and that for the first time they would have specialist teachers for some of their subjects. They seemed quite excited, and I hoped we would soon settle down to a good year's work. I gave out their exercise books for the subjects I would be teaching and for the first time they had a timetable to put on the inside of the desk lids. Then it was playtime and I told those girls who had been in J3 to look after the rest and show them where the playground and toilets were.

    I went to the Staff Room and was glad of my coffee. The staff had attended a meeting the day before and all felt ready for another school year. I wondered how my daughters were getting on and found that Elizabeth was form captain this term. Rebecca was Plantagenet representative on the school council. Both were very excited, and loved their new form mistress, who was young and pretty and also gym mistress. We all looked set for a good time ahead.

CHAPTER SEVENTEEN

John was feeling absolutely fine by the last week in September, and really looking forward to taking a service again. The church was absolutely packed. Many people who do not usually attend said they had come because they had some connection, some couples had been married there, or had their babies baptised. Some had attended funerals. Granny D calls them 'four-wheel Christians' meaning they come on four wheels for baptisms, weddings and funerals. However, they were all very welcome and it was a great service. Ron, one of our own Local Preachers led the service and John preached. Young Benedick read the lessons, and Granny D, as our oldest member led the prayers of intercession.

We had our usual tea and coffee after the service and people chatted, but there was a difference. This was the last time we would worship in the church that had been here for over a hundred years.

One lady took John aside and told him that during the service she had had an idea.

"Why not let us buy a hymnbook, and start the new building with a new set? She thought people would be willing to pay far more than a new hymnbook would cost.

John stopped the chatter and told them what had been suggested. There was loud applause. So Derek and the other stewards quickly collected piles of hymnbooks, and asked who would like to buy one, to have something from the old church.

Everyone present wanted one, and some wanted two or three for presents. The outcome was that all the books were cleared and a substantial amount was added to the funds. It was a very popular idea.

John was asked to lock the church and lots of photographs were taken. John pocketed the key, and told me he was going to suggest that it be put in a glass box to hang in the new church. Another good idea, I thought.

Over lunch, we were chatting as usual, when Rebecca said

"Dad, this will give us a chance to buy the new hymnbook which is just about to be published. We would be very up to date."

"Of course," said John, 'Hymns and Psalms'."

Elizabeth frowned thoughtfully and said

"I noticed in The Methodist Recorder that The British Methodist Youth Choir were offering to give a concert introducing some of the new hymns. Why not invite them to come to us. Proceeds would help the Building Fund."

John told her it was a brilliant idea, and that he would talk it over with the Stewards.

Next day the noise began. And what a noise it was. The first lorry arrived soon after eight in the morning, and we were thankful to go to school. I couldn't imagine how they would actually begin. Would they remove the roof first?

I never knew. When we returned from school the lot was demolished and lying in a cloud of dust.

We had been careful to close all our windows and doors, but we had not escaped. A thick layer of brick dust lay everywhere.

We all went to inspect the site and found quite a crowd of people inspecting the rubble. One passer-by had known nothing about the church closing, and was very upset. She thought vandals had done it. Someone else thought a bomb had gone off. We re-assured them, but it caused quite a stir.

Elizabeth and Rebecca started looking through the rubbish for nice bricks. They picked out about a dozen and brought them in to wash.

John had not anticipated the mess it would make in the Manse, and told me he would get a firm of cleaners in to go through the house. When Derek heard about it he said.

"Quite right, and the church will pay. What's more we have booked you all in for three nights at 'The Basket Maker.' I suggest John comes to us during the day whilst you are all at school."

I must say I was very thankful. I felt I was breathing brick dust.

After three days, the professional cleaners came in and did a brilliant job. We moved back home and John was able to start work again.

The firm buying the bricks to refurbish the Docks was very quick and efficient. The bricks, including all the rubble were loaded into waiting lorries and driven off.

The empty site now looked enormous. I could now see that there would be room for all the houses around a green area as well as a church.

The next Sunday Services were held at Stepping Stones, they had a large hall and our Stewards had set out chairs on two sides of an aisle. A table had to serve as a lectern, but we had flowers, collecting plates, and the Bible to make us feel at home. Hymns had been printed on A4 sheets and everyone who came said how much they had enjoyed the service. One lady said.

"I don't know what I expected, but it was quite all right. It's not the building that makes a church, it's the people."

John heartily agreed with her and said she had better come and hear next week's sermon which he was working on. This was about Stewardship and its title would be 'What is a Church?'

The children had been able to meet in the classrooms, and refreshments had been served, using the school kitchen. We would be quite comfortable for the next few weeks. John hoped it wouldn't be months, but nobody knew.

Charlotte Anne and Richard told John they would like him to baptise the triplets in the new church. They had asked to have my baptismal hymn, and the godparents were going to be the same for all three babies. Our girls were the godmothers, and Richard's brother Mark was their godfather. Peter John and Vanessa were also godparents.

"Do you want us to share the service with Peter John and Vanessa, and have Alexandra baptised at the same time, or do you think they will want their own service?" Richard asked.

John said he would ask them, and do whichever they preferred. He thought it might be a bit awkward to do a joint service. It could get a bit messy moving four babies about.

"But if that is what you all want, I'm sure it can be arranged," he assured him.

John spent a lot of time on his 'Stewardship' service and I'm sure he was glad of a quiet house to himself whilst we were at school.

We were all settling down to the new school year, and a different timetable. Both Elizabeth and Rebecca were entered for music examinations in November. They were both working hard at their instruments, and determined to get good marks.

Rebecca was also very excited for we had managed to buy a trampoline, which was now installed in the garden. We all had a turn on it, but none of us was anything like Rebecca's standard. We just jumped up and down and were glad to stay upright. She could do all sorts of acrobatics including somersaults.

Elizabeth told us that her sister was really good, even better than the other girls who went to 'Gloucester Springers.'

The girls were both excited about the new play chosen by Mrs. Hazelbury for this year's production. It was 'Anne of Green Gables'.

Who was going to be 'Anne'? Mrs. Hazelbury had had a word with me in the Staff Room.

"Your girls would be my first choice," she said, "but it wouldn't be fair to the others to give them the main parts again. So what I have decided to do is let the girls choose all the parts. They know each other well now, and I trust them to choose the right girls for all the parts. We will vote on it."

"But there is something else I want to talk to you about. Last year your girls asked me if the Special School could be invited to our dress rehearsal. They explained that you had written a play for their Sunday School, and that it all went very well.

"Yes" I explained "it was called 'The Most Beautiful Story of All' and it took children to different book lands, finishing with the Christmas story, from the Bible of course."

"How would you feel about our little ones doing it for their Christmas play?"

I told her I would bring a copy in for her to read.

"If you like it and think it would be all right, then of course you can produce it. I would be delighted."

I gave Judy, as I called Mrs. Hazelbury, a copy of my play and told her I would help in any way I could if she chose to use it.

At the end of the week there was great excitement. Elizabeth and Rebecca had been voted as first choice for the part of 'Anne', taking two nights each as they had for 'Alice'.

"There was no objection from anyone," Judy told me. "All the girls realised they were the obvious choice as they had the right colour hair, could speak and act well, and no-one in the audience would know it wasn't the same girl.

All the other main parts had been well chosen. Marilla, Matthew and Mrs.Lynde were obvious choices. Diana was not so easy as there were several girls who fitted the part. These had been asked to read the part, and then it was apparent who played the part most realistically.

I congratulated our two on being chosen again for the principal part, and said I hoped no one had thought it was favouritism. They assured me that this was not the case.

"No-one knew who anyone else was voting for, so how could they think that. Mrs. Hazelbury didn't know who had been chosen, for she tipped all the papers onto the table and picked three girls to sort it out," said Rebecca.

"Only two other girls had a vote for the part of 'Anne'," Elizabeth said. "And they are going to be our deputies. Everyone else voted for us and said how pleased they were."

"Just as a matter of interest" I smiled at them, "who did you two suggest?"

They giggled and confessed they had voted for each other.

"Sam is playing Diana and Kate is Marilla," Elizabeth said. "Guess who is Mrs. Lynde?"

"I couldn't possibly guess" I said, "You will have to tell me."

"Sarah," they both smiled.

"She is thrilled to bits to be chosen, and she is just right for the part," said Rebecca. "It won't matter if she can't pronounce some of her words properly. It all adds to the part." We all agreed.

"It shouldn't take either of you long to learn your words," I said. "You know the book so well. Who wrote the play for you?"

"The sixth form girls who are taking Drama for 'A' level" Elizabeth informed me. "And it's brilliant."

"I think I would like to do Drama at 'A' level," Rebecca said, "and don't think it's an easy option. It would be very hard work."

"I'm sure it would" I assured her. "But that is a long way off, and you may change your mind lots of times before then."

CHAPTER EIGHTEEN

I soon got used to my new Transition Form, and the day before we broke up for the October half term I invited my five boarders to come home for their evening meal. I had left a Meat and Potato Pie in the Aga, with baked apples stuffed with dates to follow.

They enjoyed themselves and then went up with our two to the attic bedrooms where there were board games and jigsaws to keep them happy, while I washed up. I asked them if they would fancy doing some practical chemistry afterwards. They looked puzzled; as well they might, until Elizabeth explained that this meant making fudge. They were delighted. They chose cherry fudge and took some back to share with the other boarders. Only the farmers' daughters were going home for half term. The others lived too far away. One girl lived in the Falkland Islands.

They were not upset about it, for they knew that they would have a good time in the Boarding House. There were to be two coach trips, one to The Bull Ring at Birmingham so they could do some Christmas shopping, and one to an Adventure Playground.

We of course, were looking forward to seeing our grandchildren again. We had one day with Peter John and Vanessa, although we didn't see much of Peter John; Banks do not have half-term holidays. Alexandra was growing rapidly and was trying to sit up. Her favourite game was throwing things to the floor and watching someone picking them up for her. I noticed she was enjoying her rattle, although sometimes she bumped her head with it. She didn't seem to worry.

Emma loved her baby sister and always got a smile from her when she played with her on her mat. She called our two 'Bisbuf' and 'Beca.' Alexandra was still 'Lexi'. Our two enjoyed playing with Emma and reading to her. She loved all her books, and had lots of them, but her favourite was 'Winnie the Pooh'. Her favourite Teddy was the one John and I had given to her the Christmas before she was born. Now she would soon be two and was speaking very well.

John mentioned the baptismal service. Vanessa said they had talked about it, and thought it would be fun to share the service with the triplets. The only trouble was that they didn't want to wait too long. Neither in fact did Charlotte Anne and Richard. John told them that he couldn't promise that the new church would be ready whilst the babies were still tiny, but what about a different church.

"I have five more churches in Gloucester," he said.

They said they would contact Charlotte Anne and Richard and see what they thought about it. We saw the two little girls bathed and put to bed and then came home.

Two days later we drove to Birmingham. This time John drove and we arrived in time for coffee. The little ones were all asleep in their baskets and we saw at once how much they had grown.

Jonathan was sucking his thumb, Claire had, as usual, kicked her shawl off and smiled as soon as she woke up. Daniel was just sleeping peacefully and looked thoroughly contented. Charlotte Anne was managing to feed all three, and they were obviously thriving. They all weighed over seven pounds, and everyone was very pleased with their progress.

Charlotte Anne showed us the pram they had chosen. A large pushchair, which could be folded and put in the car. It held all three. Two side by side, and one slightly in front.

"Claire likes to sit in front." Charlotte Anne explained. She can see more. It was quite large of course and took up a lot of room in the hall.

Richard was working, but left a message to say we were all invited to lunch in the hospital dining room, where he would join us. Charlotte Anne took her car with the three little seats arranged in a row at the back. Elizabeth sat beside her, and Rebecca would take her turn on the return journey.

The babies were very popular amongst the hospital staff, and made quite a fuss of. We had a good meal and whilst we were having our coffee Carey came to join us.

She was now in her second year of training and enjoying it very much. At present she was on the Maternity Ward. She had said that she would like to do her Midwifery training when she had finished her course. She told us now that she had changed her mind.

"They don't really need nursing," she said. "It's good in the labour ward, but after birth the mums take over, except at night, of course. We do get a chance to feed the babies and give them a cuddle then."

Elizabeth was listening carefully. "I thought after general training I would go to Queen Charlottes and do Midwifery, then go to Great Ormond Street to do my children's nursing."

"I thought that too," Carey said, "but not now."

"What has changed your mind, and what are you thinking of specialising in?" I asked her.

"At the moment I'm working in the Renal Wards and loving it. Next I go to Oncology and I think that will be fascinating too. We'll just have to see. All I do know is, that I love nursing."

Carey had to go back to work, but took little Claire's chair to the car for us. I carried Jonathan and John carried Daniel. They were beginning to let us know that it was now their dinnertime.

When feeding and changing time was finished, Charlotte Anne brought out some details of houses they had been looking at. They were all fairly new and had been built on the hospital campus. The one they liked best was a four bedroom detached house.

"That is our first choice" Charlotte Anne told us, "but we are not sure we can afford it. It would give us plenty of room. We thought the boys could share a bedroom and Claire could have the smallest room. That would still give us a spare room for guests."

There was a large fitted kitchen and a very large living room. Whilst we were admiring it there was a telephone call from Richard.

Charlotte Anne came in looking extremely happy.

"Richard has just been told he has a big promotion. He is no longer a junior doctor, but a houseman. He says we can easily afford our dream house and we will get on to the authorities as soon as he comes home."

We were able to leave them feeling very happy. We had talked about the baptismal service over lunch. They agreed that John should arrange a service in one of the local churches for an afternoon next month. Alexandra would be four months old and the triplets just three months old. We all looked forward to it.

When we arrived home John listened to his answer phone. The only urgent call was from Pam. She was to have her operation at the end of next week and begin her treatment soon after. I rang her and told her about our arrangements and she said that would give her something to look forward to.

"Will it be all right if we bring Millie to the service?" she said. "I would love you to see her now, she looks really bonny."

I assured her that we would love to see her, and we hoped lots of our church family would feel they could come to the service.

Elizabeth said "Invite them to tea after the service."

Rebecca laughed and said "Do that, and you'll have crowds then from all over the Circuit."

John said, "Just give me time to get the church booked. The stewards would not be at all happy if people tell them they are coming, when they know nothing about it."

We were soon back to school, and preparations for the two school productions were organised. The little ones were very excited about their play 'The Most Beautiful Story of All.' Parts were given out and learned and rehearsals began.

The babies in J1 had no trouble learning lines, they all knew the nursery rhymes and enjoyed singing them. J2 who were four or five years old loved being characters from their storybooks. Their teacher told them that she was looking for good behaviour as well as good reading, before choosing people to send to Mrs. Hazelbury.

The school took boys up to seven years old as well as girls, and they all wanted to be Thomas the tank engine. Jackie Jones their teacher told me she had never had such good behaviour.

"Long may it last" she said.

J3 and J4 were responsible for providing actors for longer speaking parts, and Transition would provide the main parts and the characters in 'Learning Land'

They were all on stage for the final scene 'The Nativity' and bigger children had been chosen for Mary and Joseph.

Mrs. Hazelbury did not usually take drama lessons with anyone under ten years old, so she was glad of help from their teachers.

'Anne of Green Gables' was well under way. Our two knew their parts by the end of the half-term holiday and were looking forward to rehearsals.

The art department had taken on the scenery for both plays, and were very busy painting large boards to fit the stage.

The senior school, years three, four and five, were busy rehearsing for a Shakespeare play, which was put on jointly with the boys from 'King's School'.

This year it was 'Midsummer Night's Dream' and was to be given two nights in our school and two more at 'Kings.'

The two schools joined, not only in 'The Literary Society' but also had a joint 'Orchestral Society.' The two sixth forms also had social evenings, which raised money for charity.

This year, our profits from the two productions were going to 'The Pied Piper Appeal,' which is for our local Special Care Baby Unit. We all hoped we would sell lots of tickets and make a large amount for them.

We were getting quite used to worshipping in our temporary accommodation, and we were pleased to find that some of the staff and mums from the school came and joined us. One of the mums told John that she found it easier in the school.

"Church buildings make me feel uneasy," she said.

John told her that he hoped the new church, which was now being built, would be more welcoming for her. She was not alone in finding traditional churches strange. I remembered Mum telling me, not long before she died, that after speaking at a women's meeting, one of the ladies present had said,

"I would love to go to church, but I never know how to behave."

I remembered my reply was "I would feel like that in a bookmakers."

It is strange to those of us who have grown up with church as a big part of our lives, but if you had never been, it must seem strange.

Knowing when to stand up, or should you kneel for prayers. Everyone else seems to know exactly what to do.

In a school it was different; the building was familiar to start with. John said

"Just entering the door could be very off-putting, to some." He would give this a lot of thought and see what could be done about making the new church 'more friendly' to strangers.

We had a call from Charlotte Anne and Richard telling us about their new house. They had put down their deposit and arranged a mortgage. They hoped they could be in before Christmas. It was all very exciting for them. We also congratulated Richard on his promotion. He explained that it had come much sooner than he had expected. The Consultant he worked for was going abroad to work somewhere in India in a very poor area. His Registrar had been appointed in his place and stipulated that he wanted Richard for his houseman. This meant a big rise in salary and so enabled them to buy the bigger house. We were all delighted for them.

Then he had another idea to put to John.

"In our church we have a Christingle Service on the first Sunday in December at 3pm. Well, our minister Helen has made a mistake and double booked herself for a wedding in one of our other churches. I told her about our Baptismal problem. I asked if it were possible, and you agreed, for you to take her Christingle Service and baptise our babies at the same time. She agreed with pleasure and says she will be in touch with you. What do you think?"

John said, "Let me look at my diary and I'll get back to you."

"This could be the answer" he smiled at us as he explained what Richard had said.

"I have a morning service of course, but that will be over by 11.30am. If we have an early lunch we could get away in time couldn't we? I'll have to see what Peter John and Vanessa think though."

"See what they say," I said. "If they agree, we will not have an early lunch as you suggest. We will have it on the motorway. No clearing up to do."

"Good idea" John agreed. "I'll get on to the family and see how they feel about travelling up to Birmingham."

Peter John and Vanessa agreed. "I love Christingle services," Vanessa said. "I used to love taking part, and of course I come from Birmingham so it will be like going home to me; and mum and dad will be delighted."

John looked up the telephone number of Charlotte Anne and Richard's minister and rang her. Helen Seymour was delighted.

"You will get me out of a hole" she laughed. "It is a long standing tradition in this church to hold a Christingle Service for charity on the first Sunday afternoon in December. Everybody knows that, but unfortunately they forgot to mention it to me."

"But it always happens," they assured me. "My crystal ball isn't working," I told them, "so how was I supposed to know?"

"Easily done" John assured her, and then told her of our problems with four grandchildren to baptise and no church to do it in.

"I have never held a Christingle service," John explained, but it sounds exciting, I must have a chat with you about it."

Helen kindly invited us to a meal with her. "I might just get back from my wedding in time to see these famous babies baptised" she said.

So our baptism service was to be on the first Sunday in December at 3.o.clock during the Christingle service. We were told there was always a tea party afterwards, and that all our family and friends would be very welcome. So that solved the problem of making arrangements for our family and congregation. They were all invited.

CHAPTER NINETEEN

We explained to our church family the reason for going to Birmingham to have our babies baptised. Fortunately they all understood. They were highly amused for the reason, and told us many tales of past ministers getting their diaries muddled. John is so organised that I cannot see it ever happening to him. He has to be careful, of course. He puts everything into his diary immediately and he only has one diary. Some ministers have two, one for church affairs and a private family one. He knew one minister who had one for each of his churches. Disastrous.

John always uses his diary pencil to write in details. When the date is confirmed, he inks it in. Then he immediately writes the details on to our family calendar; which hangs on the wall in the kitchen. It is very useful to me as I can work out where John is if I need him urgently. It is also a double check, and I cannot see us ever having a muddle. Providing the church authorities inform him of their traditions, of course.

Many of our church family said they would love to come to the service and suggested that John cancel the evening service here.

The Junior School had their production in the last week of November. All went extremely well. The tickets were sold out for all three nights and a nice amount would be sent to The Pied Piper Appeal. The school caretaker, whom the children all call 'Mr.Fixit,' gladly transported Dobbin for the final rehearsal and back again after the production.

'Anne of Green Gables' was to be later in December, just before we broke up. Tickets were selling well and everyone involved was looking forward to it. Charlotte Anne said

"We can hardly come with three babies" but we would love to have seen it. Is it possible to have it videoed?"

We checked with Judy Hazelbury, and then arranged for it to be videoed. She thought it would be a good idea, as there were bound to be people who couldn't attend for one reason or another. Our friend from church who had videoed Charlotte Anne's and Richard's wedding, said he would love to oblige. Then he suggested that he could copy some for sale and it might bring in quite a sum for the funds. In the end he videoed both productions and very popular they were.

On the first Sunday of December we were all up early and dressed in our best clothes. Firstly we went to our 10.30.am.service in the school, which was packed. John invited anyone who would like to come to our Baptismal service at 3 o' clock, which would include the Christingle, and explained how to get there.

Peter John and Vanessa had said they would pick Dad up and look after him for the day. We went home for a quick tidy up and a drink of coffee and then left in plenty of time to have lunch on the motorway.

We arrived at the church and found the family waiting for us. There was a lovely surprise, as John's parents and sister had come with their families.

My brothers and their families were there and so were lots of our church family, including Pam and Derek, with their daughter and son-in-law and little Millie.

I was able to have a lovely cuddle with Millie, who was a little charmer and full of fun. John had been asked where he would like the Christingle money to go, as he was taking the service. He thought long and hard about it and then decided it should go to 'The Cystinosis Society.'

"I hope people will take an interest and ask what it is all about." He explained.

They certainly did. One lady came to find out more about it, and explained that she was assistant editor of one the big national newspapers.

"I will write an article about it" she said as she was introduced to Millie and her parents.

The service was delightful. As the first carol 'Once in Royal David's City' was sung, the children who had been collecting money for charity, came forward to collect their Christingles. These were displayed on large trays at the front and looked very attractive. A large orange to represent the world, with a candle lit to represent Christ the light of the world. Four cocktail sticks threaded with sweets to represent the good gifts we receive. A red ribbon tied around the orange symbolised that God's gifts were for all.

Then we sang 'We light a candle to your name' and the children returned to their seats. John suggested that the candles should be blown out for safety reasons. Some of the girls had long hair, and we all had a few anxious moments when the flame appeared to come too close.

John then explained where the money the children had collected was going. Having got permission from her parents, he told them about little Millie and how we all hoped for a cure for this dreadful condition.

Then it was time to baptise our grandchildren. Firstly, Alexandra Katy. The girls and I took a triplet each, so Charlotte Anne and Richard could go and support Peter John and Vanessa as godparents. Peter John held Emma, whilst Vanessa held Alexandra. John baptised his granddaughter and gave her back to her Mother. Then Emma caused some amusement as she held out her arms to her grandpa.

John took her and explained to one and all that he had baptised Emma when she was a few months old. However she wasn't going to be left out so he blessed her, before handing her back to her Daddy. She was quite satisfied.

Then John asked Charlotte Anne and Richard to bring their triplets to be baptised. I took Emma and Carey Jane came to look after Alexandra.

A large party surrounded the font. Charlotte Anne carried Claire, Elizabeth carried Jonathan and Rebecca held Daniel. Emma was determined not to be left out. She slipped out of my arms and ran to stand between her parents. Richard's brother Mark made everyone laugh when he said to Charlotte Anne

"You could have made it quads so I had a baby to hold."

When everyone was organised John baptised the babies in the order in which they were born, Jonathan Mark, Daniel William and Claire Louise.

Then we sang my baptismal hymn, to the tune 'Away in a Manger.' It was very appropriate for the first Sunday in Advent.

After the service there were refreshments for everyone in the school hall. All the babies needed feeding and changing, so the mums were shown into the vestry and there were plenty of people to help with changing.

The Rev.Helen Seymour arrived during the afternoon and admired all our grandchildren. She delighted Emma by giving her a Christingle to take home. She told John how grateful she was to him for getting her out of a problem, and suggested that he come again sometime for a special service.

We managed to talk to all our family and I was glad to see Dad looking a little more like himself. He had a word with my brothers and suggested a family photograph.

"I want to show off my wonderful family to my friends at 'Westerley'" he said. And so it was arranged.

CHAPTER TWENTY

The photograph taken at the baptism was beautiful, and of course it included both Vanessa's and Richard's parents, as well as his brother Mark. I immediately ordered framed copies, and they would be Christmas presents for one and all.

'Anne of Green Gables' went without a hitch and everyone seemed to enjoy it. One of the parents had spoken to Mrs. Jenner, and told her he was so impressed that he would make an extra donation for 'The Pied Piper' appeal.

The local press had been invited and there were some lovely photographs of the production.

Both Elizabeth and Rebecca had taken grade three music exams and there was much rejoicing when they both received Honours. Elizabeth rang Miss Greenwood and she was delighted. She had been to see their production, for we had sent her two tickets for the final night. She told us how proud she was of Elizabeth, and that she would follow her career with interest.

Dad was delighted that both of them had gained Honours, and told us how he would boast to his friends. "Who else has children, grandchildren and great grandchildren like me?" he asked proudly.

We told him that there were lots of people who were just as proud of their families. Then we told him we would fetch him in time for all our Christmas activities.

John was now spending a lot of time talking to Stewards and the Architect, about the new building. Sebastian Webster, who had designed most of the new houses on the estate, was a wonderful help. He had offered at an early meeting to freely give his time and expertise as his contribution to the church. It was much appreciated. He seemed to agree with John and all the stewards on most things concerning the building. It must be welcoming, and easily converted from chapel to meeting room.

There was much discussion about colour schemes for chairs as well as walls. Heating, it had been agreed would be under floor. There must also be a good sound system. People of all ages had been asked for their opinions, but it was the young peoples suggestion of colour scheme, which had the biggest vote. The walls and woodwork were to be in very pale turquoise. The chairs were to be in different shades of pale blue and turquoise. The carpet tiles would be in a deeper shade. The family who had given the pews in the old church were very enthusiastic about the colours.

"Just like the colours in the sea" Mary smiled.

Another question was broached. "What about having screens?" There was no agreement, about this.

"I do not want to watch television when I come to worship" came from the majority of people. Some of the younger ones were in favour, but they were over-ruled, and there was no further discussion.

Sebastian thought it was a shame. "They will want it in a few years and it will be much more expensive to install, although not impossible." He was outvoted.

The plans Sebastian Webster had offered were carefully studied. Firstly by the Circuit Stewards, then Church Stewards and were displayed each Sunday for all to see.

John explained that they would be displayed in his study, and anyone who wanted a closer and longer look would be welcome to come and see them.

Another item much discussed, was the name of the new church. Should it just be Cotteswold Methodist Church or should it have a name?

One member at a meeting suggested that as John had done such a lot of work it should be called St. John's. There was much hilarity, but John declined, reminding them that the Circuit already had a St. John's.

St. Andrew's was another suggestion, "because he brought people to Jesus." However it was an idea from Benedick, which won the day. "I think 'Christchurch' would be the best name. That says it all." There was a great applause and it was carried unanimously.

'Christchurch Cotteswold' it would be.

The second Sunday in December was when our Stewardship Campaign was to be launched, and John had spent many hours preparing the service. He was very keen that everyone connected with us in any way, should feel some responsibility for the new church.

He had often heard the phrase "Somebody should do something," now he wanted to say "Maybe you are that someone."

Many people think Stewardship means giving money. It does of course, but how much should people give? There are people who think that when the collection plate comes they can sort out their change and give some of it. John wanted everyone to realise that their giving should be thought about carefully.

There are some, mostly older people, who think that a tenth of their income is what they should give. That is not always the right thing to do. Some have a large mortgage and other commitments. Everyone should think for himself or herself, what they consider to be their duty, and then give it regularly.

Every Methodist church has a commitment to the Circuit, for it is the Circuit which pays the Minister, and his expenses such as travelling, pension etc. So a charge is made for each member. That is taken before anything is left for the local church. Therefore there is an obligation for each member to pay more than the Circuit Assessment. This of course, changes each year, but it is a guide to deciding weekly giving.

Stewardship is about far more than money, of course. It means good use of our time and talents. Not everyone can preach, or look after the money, but all have some talents and these should be used for the good of all.

John chose his hymns carefully, as he does for any service. Young Benedick read the lessons very well, and John had asked him whether he felt he could tell the congregation of his hopes for his future. He agreed. So he finished reading the Gospel, and then told everyone that he was offering to train as a local preacher and hoped to begin his studies in the New Year.

After the service, there was a short meeting to distribute forms for all who wished to take one. This was so people could think about their commitments and then offer their time, their talents, and their money for the good of the church. Their new church. 'Christchurch'.

Derek told a delighted John that he would need more forms. The ones provided were all taken and more were requested.

"The amazing thing is, John, that people who do not normally come to worship have taken forms." Some were connected with 'Stepping Stones' who had generously allowed us to use the school for worship. Others were parents of children in our uniformed organisations. Some had come because they had seen the bare patch where our church had stood and wondered what was happening.

The amazing thing was that the congregation meeting for worship had increased significantly, and many of these people had requested forms. One lady said

"Your minister really made me think. I have so much to be thankful for and I had better do something about it."

We could only wait now, and see what response there had been when the forms were returned.

The first Sunday in the New Year, Covenant Sunday, was when John was to preach a Thanksgiving Service for all that had been promised.

People had been asked to hand their completed forms back to one of the Stewards well before then, so they could be checked and responded to.

Some came back to John on the day after the service, and there was a Stewards' meeting arranged for the end of the week to assess the response.

It was overwhelming. People had really thought about how they could help, not only with their weekly giving, but also with their time and talents. One elderly lady said she hadn't much energy to do church cleaning, but could see to cleaning the silver and wash and iron the communion cloths. One really busy man with a high-powered job, offered to take the collection to the bank every Monday morning, as that was his day off.

The scouts took on the horrid job of cleaning the toilets. The guides offered to wash up after coffee on Sunday mornings. One elderly couple who were in a residential home said they couldn't offer much, but they did have time to pray, and would use each morning between breakfast and coffee time to pray for anyone who needed it.

Some retired, but able people offered their cars to bring people to church or take people who found difficulty in walking to hospital, or doctor's appointments.

The Women's Meeting ladies offered to help with distributing flowers to the sick. They also suggested starting a craft circle.

When the Treasurer and Finance Committee met to add up the giving that had been promised they were amazed and delighted.

John had told them he didn't want to know who had promised, but just the overall amount. He was so amazed he told them they had better check the amount again.

He was assured that it had been checked, and double-checked. When the amount of gift aiding had been added, the total monthly giving came to more than twice the previous amount. This would mean the church could fulfil all its obligations, and have enough left over to give to those in need. What a blessing.

John felt he could relax a little and give his mind to the Service of Thanksgiving on Covenant Sunday.

We had organised our usual buffet for Boxing Day for the family and another, later in the week, for our 'Thank You' buffet.

Charlotte Anne and Richard said they were bringing the babies both to the buffet and to the Thanksgiving Service.

"They might as well get used to our sort of hectic life from the beginning" Richard said. Charlotte Anne said one mother had asked her if she thought it was safe to take the babies into crowds, with all the germs around. Charlotte Anne had told her that they were not delicate babies, and like all children needed to build up their immune systems. They were all three used to being bundled into the car and taken about. They attended their mother and baby group, and also went into the crèche on Sunday mornings. Someone asked her how on earth she managed to carry all three around.

"Quite easily" she smiled "I put them one at a time into their push chair, then wheel it to the garage. Once I have the car on the drive I put Claire into her car seat and strap her in. Follow with her brothers, and then fold up the pushchair and put it in the boot. Drive to wherever I am going and then do everything in reverse order. It really is quite simple. As long as they are fed and changed regularly, they enjoy the attention they receive from everyone." They are all happy babies and love being talked to.

We are very proud of the way all our grandchildren are being brought up, and love them to bits. Emma is a very busy little girl. She goes to the nursery her church runs twice a week for toddlers. She also goes to Baby Ballet and a musical group where they play drums and other noisy instruments and sing action songs. Lexi enjoys it all as much as she does.

We fetched Dad during the week before Christmas. John was just too busy, but I took the girls. On the way home Dad asked what was happening on Christmas Day itself. We told him that as usual, we would have Midnight Communion followed by the usual Christmas morning service, which was at 'Stepping Stones' this year. Then after a light lunch we would have a rest, followed by a walk with the dogs. Then we will have Christmas Dinner about 6.pm.

"I just wondered whether you would like to go to 'The Tara' for Christmas Dinner? It would be my Christmas present to you all," he said

We were very grateful, but said we would talk it over with John when we got back.

"Well, it's like this" Dad said. "I cannot face Christmas shopping, so I thought I would give everyone money. I thought Christmas dinner out would save you a lot of work, but if you would rather not, then will it be all right to give you money, and you can spend it how you like?"

We assured him that it would be wonderful, and we would probably use it to have a day off sometime in the New Year. The girls both told their Grandpa that they would love to have the money to spend on clothes or books. They just love shopping.

Dad was quite content. As far as his present was concerned, he would have a photograph, like everyone else, but my brothers and their families had joined with us to buy him a video machine, and some lovely tapes of classical music, showing views of various beauty spots. He doesn't get around much now and spends holidays with the family, but he loves music and the countryside and will enjoy these tapes.

I had already ordered and paid for our turkey, beef and ham for all our Christmas meals, so we declined Dad's kind offer, but told him we would have a nice meal out when we could get away for a day.

'Stepping Stones' school had kindly left up the Christmas decorations for us to enjoy. The Midnight Communion service was absolutely packed. The collection always goes to charity, and this year we were pleased to give it to the school that had been so generous to us.

Christmas morning service was also well attended and we went home to buffet lunch. Nick and Caroline had arrived in time for this. They both looked so happy, and Caroline proudly showed us her beautiful ring. It was a large ruby surrounded by diamonds.(Arsenal colours, of course). It also matched her beautiful red velvet dress.

John and I had given them their copy of the photograph taken at the baptismal service, and a beautiful Cedar Wood fruit bowl. We had bought this from a wood turner at a local craft fair. Elizabeth and Rebecca filled it with fruit and nuts. It looked gorgeous, and Nick and Caroline were delighted with it.

After lunch, John was sent up for a rest and Dad also was in need of an hour or so in bed. The girls helped me clear up and then went to their rooms to enjoy their presents.

We didn't get our walk, as we had a surprise visit from Derek and Pam. Pam had just finished her treatment and was feeling fit and healthy, but that wasn't the reason for the visit.

Apparently, after Midnight Communion, a stranger had come up to one of the Stewards and asked to speak to the Treasurer. Derek had been brought to him and been given a bag containing a lot of money. The man told Derek it was a 'thank offering' to be used for our new church. He wouldn't give his name, but said he had been at a very low ebb in hospital earlier in the year, and John had been a tremendous help to him.

"Now" he said, "because of the help I received, I was able to face a very big operation and I am cured."

"I haven't counted the money," Derek said. "I thought I would bring it straight round and let you know."

John was very surprised, but said he knew whom it must be. "I didn't do much, just talked to him and he seemed to be grateful."

"But I thought you were supposed to be resting?" Derek laughed "Oh John what are we going to do with you?"

Then the two men went into the study to count the money. It was one thousand pounds in fifty pound notes. They brought the money in to show us. None of us had seen a fifty pound note before. Dad was certainly intrigued, as were the rest of us.

John said he would get onto the hospital authorities, and try to find out the man's name and address.

"All I know is his name is Ptolemy. I had never met anyone of that name before. That is why I remember it."

The money was put in the safe, and would be banked as soon as banks opened again. What a wonderful gesture.

Later I asked John about the man he had helped.

"You were in a private room, and not allowed to wander about, so how did he come to talk to you?"

"Well, it was when I was allowed to walk about a bit on the last day or two. I went into the loo, and there was this man just coming out and looking as though he had been given a death sentence. I just said "Hello, everything all right?" He shook his head and I could see he was close to tears. I told him who I was and said, "If you want to talk, come to my room. I gave him my room number and left it at that."

"The day I was told I could come home he came in and told me about his problems. I just listened and gave him my opinion about his best course of action. I told him I would pray for him, and asked if he would like to be put on the church prayer list. That is all I did, except to ask him his name.

He just said "I'm Ptolemy."

"How are you going to be able to thank him?" I asked.

"All I can do is talk to the hospital authorities, they will not be able to give me his name and address; that is confidential. I will write a letter. They, or one of the chaplains, may agree to post it on to him. I certainly hope so."

Boxing Day was a wonderful, but noisy day. With a happy toddler and four babies to look after we were all kept busy. Charlotte Anne and Vanessa used our bedroom for feeding and changing, but there were plenty of offers to cuddle, and our girls kept Emma happy with her toys. Nick and Caroline received plenty of congratulations, and Caroline loved helping with the babies. Toffee and Fudge thoroughly enjoyed all the petting they received, as well as the crumbs dropped from biscuits and cakes.

Richard came into the kitchen, where Caroline and I were putting out cakes and biscuits for an afternoon snack, and said he wanted to ask us a big favour. They were moving into their new house in the New Year.

"Do you think I could bring Charlotte Anne and the babies here whilst I get it all done?" he asked. I was delighted and told him they could stay overnight.

"Why don't you see to the removal then come and join them here and take them back next day into their new home?"

Caroline said. "This is such an exciting family I'm coming into. I never know what is going to happen next." We all laughed. Of course we are all used to it, and think every new happening is normal, but someone like Caroline from a quiet and very small family, finds it all quite extraordinary." However, we waved them all off to their own homes, and settled down to a quiet evening. We hoped.

Two days later we held our buffet to say 'Thank You' for the work people did week by week. The Guides were still offering to do jobs, so they could send money to their favourite overseas charity. Our girls we among them of course, and they were all a great help. They were very efficient in laying out the food, and serving it. Then they helped themselves to their share and finally cleared up, leaving everything tidy.

New Year was the next excitement and John was excused all domestic duties again, so he could think about his Covenant Service, which this year was also a Thanksgiving for all that had been offered.

This was the first indication to most folk about what there was to be thankful for.

The service began with the Hymn 'God is here as we his people,' and what a sound there was. The screens, which divided the hall from two classrooms, had to be drawn back, and there was still a crush.

John had asked the Architect and the Treasurer to read the lessons and various other people took part. We had a solo, and two people led the prayers of intercession.

John's sermon was superb. There was no shuffling or fidgeting, everyone was really listening. When John said Amen at the end, Derek got up from his seat and amazed us all by saying.

"I want to quote from scripture."

'There was a man sent from God whose name was John."

"We have just been given several reasons to thank God for our new church. I think we can truly say 'Thank you' God for sending John to us." Then he looked at our family and said. "You must be very proud of him."

There was yet another surprise. Dad got up, and collecting Claire from me, went to the front and said.

"Thank you Derek. As the eldest and the youngest members of this family we want to say, on behalf of us all, that we are truly proud, and feel immensely privileged, to be members of

'The Minister's Family'

The congregation rose to sing our final hymn. We lustily sang. 'Now thank we all our God.'